Defiant
HEIR

USA TODAY BESTSELLING AUTHOR
MICHELLE HEARD

Cover Designer: Sybil Wilson, <u>PopKitty Design</u>

Cover Model: COOPER

Photographer Credit: <u>Wander Book Club Photography</u>

TABLE OF CONTENTS

Dedication

Donita, you inspire me with your strength.

Thank you for sharing your story with me. You were a godsend with this book. Kao's story would not have been a possibility without you.

Songlist

Click here - *Spotify*

Synopsis

The man of my dreams is nothing short of perfect. Kao
Reed is a hermit who loves to live in the shadows.
With striking blue eyes and a gentle nature, he won my
heart years ago. I've woven all my dreams and future
around him.

But then the worst happens.
My dreams crumble to dust, and my future becomes a bleak
wasteland.
And the man I love with all my heart becomes a stranger in
the blink of an eye.

My blind love, my blind love,
See how he fights, see how he fights,
He lost his sight, he lost his will,
He became defiant, he became heartless.
Did you ever see such a thing in your life,
As my blind love?

Defiant Heir

THE HEIRS
Book 3

College/New Adult series of interconnected STANDALONES.

*"There is beauty in everything, even in silence and darkness." — **Helen Keller.***

Family Tree

KAO REED

↓ ↓

Marcus Reed   Willow Brooks
Father   *Mother*

Godmother: Miss Sebastian

Godfather: Jaxson West

Best Friends: Noah West, Hunter Chargill & Jase Reyes

FALLON REYES

↓ ↓

Falcon Reyes   Layla Shepard
Father   *Mother*

Godmother: Kingsley Hunt

Godfather: Mason Chargill & Lake Cutler

Best friends: Hana Cutler, Jade Daniels & Mila West

My blind love, my blind love,

See how he fights, see how he fights,

He lost his sight, he lost his will,

He became defiant, he became heartless.

Did you ever see such a thing in your life,

As my blind love?

Chapter 1

KAO

Fallon 19; Kao 23

My gaze locks on Fallon as she enters the restaurant on campus. Once again, her beauty knocks the air from my lungs. I've known her all my life, and the sight of her still stuns me.

I watch as she stops by a table to talk with Summer, one of the girls on the decorating committee with her. My eyes drink in Fallon's golden-brown hair, her delicate features, her sharp gaze alight with intelligence.

When Fallon shakes her head at something Summer mentions, the corner of my mouth lifts. The girl of my dreams is nothing short of a control freak. Fallon takes care of everything at Trinity Academy as if it's second nature to her. She never misses a beat.

Where I'm the happiest moving in the shadows, the spotlight follows Fallon. Even though she seems to take after her father, she got her mother's big heart.

Fallon smiles at Summer before turning in my direction. I'm seated at our usual table that's always reserved for our group of friends.

Our eyes lock and just having her attention on me is enough to make my heartbeat speed up.

Fallon and I have always been close. I even escorted her to her prom during her senior year. At first, we were just friends, but it changed when she started attending Trinity Academy a couple of months ago.

Initially, attraction began to grow between us. I became Fallon's plus one for every event she had to attend. Now we spend most of our time together.

My gaze drifts over Fallon, and the love I have for her fills my heart to the point that it might burst from not being able to contain it. I'm addicted to the rush it gives me. Loving Fallon has become the only thing I live for. The woman is my beginning and end.

I know our friends wonder what's going on between Fallon and me, but I'm in no hurry to tell them anything. I'm a selfish bastard when it comes to her. I want to enjoy every glance, every touch, every step closer to each other before I have to share it with the world.

As Fallon takes the chair next to me, I reach a hand up and wrapping my fingers around the back of her neck, I pull her closer and press my lips to the side of her head. My eyes drift shut, and I take a deep breath of her before murmuring, "How's your day so far?"

"Good. I'm almost done arranging everything for the Christmas ball." She pulls a menu closer for us to look at. "I found a white and silver dress."

"For the ball?" I ask.

"Yeah." Her eyes flit to mine. "If you wear a charcoal suit, we'll match."

"I'll get one," I assure her. Our gazes lock, and her feelings for me make her brown irises turn to liquid gold.

Figuring I've let things linger long enough, I ask, "Are we going to go on a date at some point?"

Her eyes widen before they snap to the menu. It's only for a moment before she looks at me again. That's all it takes for Fallon to compose herself. Nothing can knock her off balance for long.

"You've taken your sweet time," she chastises me, and a smile begins to play at the corner of her mouth.

My lips pull into a grin. "Because I don't want to rush things with you." My thumb caresses her soft skin underneath her hair, and I watch how my touch makes her lips part. "I want to enjoy every moment." Fallon nods, her attention solely on me as I say, "I don't want the others to know yet."

A light frown mars her forehead. "Why?"

"I want our relationship to be ours before we have to share it with everyone."

Fallon lifts her hand to my jaw while a soft smile curves her lips. "My hermit." Her words are possessive and filled with love.

I lean closer to her and murmur, "Miss Reyes."

Her eyes lock on mine, a playful look dancing in them. "Yes, Mr. Reed."

"Will you have dinner with me tonight?"

13

Her smile turns into a happy grin. "I'd love to."

"Put me down!" Mila's voice echoes through the restaurant, and my eyes snap in her direction. I let out a chuckle when I see Jase has her tossed over his shoulder. He slaps her ass, and it has Mila laughing.

Mila's like a sister to me, and seeing her happy after the hell she's been through fills my heart with relief. Jase might be one of my best friends and Fallon's cousin, but after everything he did for Mila, he's become the pillar of our group.

I pull a little back from Fallon and glance at the menu. "What do you feel like eating?"

"I'll have the Salmon salad."

I scrunch my nose with fake disgust. I can't stomach anything that comes out of the ocean. I tried to eat prawns once, and it was almost the death of me.

I signal a waiter closer as Jase sets Mila down. She punches his shoulder with a mock angry glare while they take their seats.

"The salmon salad and a chicken sandwich," I give our orders to the waiter. When he glances up from writing the dishes down, I add, "Also, a coke and a sprite, please."

Jase and Mila add their orders, then Fallon looks at Mila. "Have you decided what to wear to the Christmas ball?"

Mila shakes her head, then Jase says, "I'm going to dress her as a sexy elf."

"Like hell you are," Mila grumbles. "It's not a costume ball."

"Damn," Jase sulks, then he glances at his cousin. "Why aren't we having a costume ball? You just took all the fun out of it."

Fallon shakes her head. "You got to dress up for Halloween. Don't mess with my plans for Christmas."

Jase lets out a chuckle. "I wouldn't dare. I don't have a death wish."

As a server brings our food, we're joined by Noah, my best friend who's more like a brother to me. Our fathers are also best friends, and we grew up really close.

"Hey," Noah mumbles while grabbing a menu, but then he looks at my plate and tells the server, "I'll have the same as him."

"How's your day?" I ask and wait for Noah to take half of my sandwich, knowing I'll get it back when his meal comes.

"Boring as fuck," Noah grumbles, then he takes a huge bite.

While I eat, I listen to the conversation around the table.

"Are we going skiing for Christmas break?" Jase asks.

I glance at Fallon, who first swallows the bite she took, then she answers, "Yeah, Kao and I are in."

The corner of my mouth lifts when Jase's eyes slant in my direction. Then he asks, "When are the two of you going to come out as a couple?"

Fallon quickly glances at me then looks back at Jase. "That, my cousin, is none of your business."

Jase lets out a chuckle. "You're not fooling anyone."

"You took forever," Mila chastises Jase. "Leave them be."

Jase's gaze turns to Mila, and a loving smile softens his features right before he frames her face with his hands and kisses her.

Fallon finishes her salad just as Noah's order comes, and it has me saying, "You can have the whole sandwich. We're going for dinner later."

"More for me," Noah grins.

I get up, and as soon as Fallon's standing, I take hold of her hand.

"Catch you all later," she says to the group before we leave the restaurant.

On our way to the dorm, we run into Hunter and Jade. They were the first of our friends to couple up. Thank God. The way they were fighting, I was afraid someone might die.

"Did you just have lunch?" Hunter asks.

"Yeah," Fallon answers. "The others are still eating, though."

Hunter and Jade continue walking toward the restaurant as Fallon and I head toward our dorm.

Entering our building, I grin down at Fallon. "Anywhere specific you want to go for dinner?"

She thinks about it as we step into the elevator, and when the doors slide shut, she answers, "The Ranch House."

Pulling my phone from my pocket, I Google their contact number, and stepping out of the elevator, I press dial. I make a reservation for seven as we walk into the suite. Tucking the device back into my pocket, I say, "All done."

"I'm going to go get ready."

Frowning, I chuckle. "But it's only two in the afternoon."

She gestures with a hand over her body. "All of this takes time, and I want to look pretty tonight. In case you haven't heard..." She takes a step closer to me until I feel her breath skim over my ear, "the guy I like finally asked me out on a date."

I let out a burst of laughter and fight not to grab hold of her so I can kiss the ever-loving crap out of her. Fallon's like fine wine. I want to savor every moment with her.

I relish in the anticipation building between us. Lifting my hand to her face, I brush my thumb slowly over her bottom lip, murmuring, "I can't wait for tonight."

Her eyes lock with mine, her expression intense and filled with excitement. "Me too."

I watch her walk to her room. It's only a matter of hours before I'll finally get to kiss her. A real fucking kiss and not the sweet pecks on the cheek and forehead I've been giving her. The corners of my mouth lift at the thought.

FALLON

I'm busy curling the ends of my hair when Hana, my best friend, comes into my room. Jase, Hana, Hunter, and I are more like family than friends. Our families go way back to when our great grandfathers were friends, and I can't imagine my life without them in it.

Hana's eyes scan over all the outfits scattered on my bed, then she asks, "Are you going somewhere?"

"Out for dinner," I say, rolling a bunch of strands around the curling iron.

Hana's eyebrows pop up. "Oh?" She moves some of the clothes out of the way then takes a seat on my bed. "With who?"

My eyes lock on my friend's face. "Kao." I watch as a slow grin spreads over her face.

"Just dinner, or *dinner*?"

Not able to hide my excitement any longer, I grin like a lovesick fool as I admit, "He finally asked me on a date."

"Damn," she gasps. "Miracles do happen."

With my attention on Hana, the curling iron presses against my jaw. It's only for a split-second before I yank it away. "Shit!" My eyes dart to the mirror, and leaning forward, I check to see if I freaking burned my face.

"What?" Hana asks.

Not seeing any marks, I mutter, "I almost burned my face." I glare at the curling iron. "Stupid thing." Remembering what we were talking about, I say, "You know Kao doesn't rush into anything. He's meticulous in everything he does."

"True."

When I'm done, I turn off the curling iron and place it on the table. I pull my fingers through my hair until I'm happy with the look.

"You're gorgeous," Hana compliments me. Rising to her feet, she says, "Let me see the complete look."

I get up from the chair and twirl in a circle for her. I've decided to wear black pants with heels, and my favorite Gucci shirt, that's black with gold writing. To round off the look, I'm wearing a taupe jacket. "So? Do you approve?"

Hana grins at me. "God, those pants make your butt look good. I'm going to steal them."

"We should go get you a pair."

"Oooh, shopping spree this weekend?" she asks.

"We can go on Sunday. I'm going to a potluck at Kao's parents on Saturday."

Hana chuckles, shaking her head. "I'll never understand you and Kao. You know everyone thinks you're a couple already?"

"Yeah," I reply as I swipe on some lipgloss. "You know I don't care what people think."

"Also true." She lets out a sigh. "As long as you're happy."

I turn to face my friend, and with a cheerful smile, I say, "I am."

"Well, you're good to go. Enjoy the evening." Hana walks to my door, and opening it, she comes face to face with Kao, who was just about to knock. "Your girl's ready," she teases him before disappearing down the hallway.

Kao steps into the room and his eyes slowly drift over me, then he murmurs, "You look beautiful, as always."

I take a moment to drink in the sight of him. He's dressed in brown chinos with a light blue, button-up shirt that does nothing to hide his muscled body.

Yum.

My gaze meets his hypnotizing blue eyes. Everyone knows I'm a control freak, but Kao's eyes are the only place I want to get lost in.

Since I discovered I had hormones, I've had a crush on him. But when I moved into the suite and I got to see him every day, it grew into love. Kao's perfect in every way. He's patient, caring, and has the kind of inner strength that makes you let down your guard. With one look, he can strip me bare.

"Hey, handsome," I say. Picking up my necklace from the table, I walk toward him. "Can you help me put this on?"

Kao nods, and once he's taken the piece of jewelry from me, I turn my back to him.

I feel his fingers skim over my skin as he moves my hair over my right shoulder, and it sends goosebumps rushing over my body. He clasps the necklace in place, and when he leans down and I feel his breath flutter over my pulse, my lips part and my eyes drift shut. His lips brush against my skin, and it makes my insides tighten.

Then he pulls back, and the moment fades as he asks, "Are you ready?"

Turning to face him, I nod. "I've been ready for years."

The corner of his mouth lifts in a hot as hell grin. "Years?"

Pushing past him, I playfully bat my eyelashes. "That's a secret I'll share with you one day."

"Hmm, I wasn't aware we were keeping secrets from each other."

I reach for his hand as I tease, "Just one."

Walking into the living room, Noah's eyes snap to us from where he was watching TV. "Drive safely."

"Always," Kao replies.

"And bring the leftovers home," Noah calls after us as we walk out the door.

"Will do."

Reaching the elevator, I ask, "Does Noah know we're going on a date?"

"I didn't tell him, but I'm sure he knows. There's not much I can hide from him," Kao answers.

We step inside as I admit, "I told Hana."

Kao lifts our joined hands, and he presses a kiss to the back of mine. "That's okay."

Walking out of the building, I hear Nate, one of the juniors, call out, "Looking good, guys."

"Thanks," I reply.

Reaching Kao's car, I wait as he opens the passenger door for me, then I climb inside. My gaze follows him when he walks around the front of the car, and then I put on my seatbelt as he slides behind the steering wheel.

We steal a moment to smile at each other before he steers the vehicle off the campus.

This is it. Finally.

"If you take highway thirty-three and then turn off on Fairview, it should get us there faster," I say.

Kao lets out a chuckle. "Yes, ma'am."

It's silent in the car for a moment, then I ask, "What made you ask me today?"

Kao glances at me. "On a date?"

I nod. "Yeah, why didn't you ask sooner?"

"Like I said earlier, I want to take things slow. I want to enjoy every moment." His gaze meets mine for a second before it returns to the road. "People are quick to rush into things, and then they miss the good part."

"The good part?" I ask.

"The falling in love part. The butterflies in your stomach. The build-up to the first kiss. You know, all the romantic things girls like."

My mouth curves up. "Could you be any more perfect?"

He lets out a chuckle. "Only in your eyes."

His answer has me asking, "Do you believe in soul mates?"

Kao thinks for a moment, then murmurs, "Two halves of one soul?"

I nod, my eyes never leaving his face.

Then he smiles at me. "Yes."

Chapter 2

FALLON

It's a nice night out, and the excitement keeps building in me as we drive to the restaurant.

My mind begins to drift, wondering if we'll have our first real kiss tonight.

God, I'm not ordering anything with garlic. Just in case.

My gaze keeps drifting to Kao's face. He's easily the most attractive man I've ever laid eyes on. His features are flawless. And his eyes – the clearest blue. They look like the heavens after it's rained, and the air is clear.

The corner of his mouth begins to lift, and his gaze darts to me. "Why do you keep staring at me?"

"It's actually unfair how attractive you are," I mutter.

Chuckling, he asks, "Why?"

"You just climb out of the shower, slap on some clothes, and you're good to go. I have to put on makeup before I dare set foot out of my bedroom, or you'll all have heart attacks." I remember the incident with the curling iron earlier and add, "I almost burned my face with the curling iron." I let out a relieved chuckle.

Kao's gaze darts to me, and it has me saying, "Luckily, I didn't burn my face off. Can you imagine that?" I roll my eyes. "Then, we'll be known as beauty and the beast." I grin at him. "With you being the beauty, of course."

"Never," he shakes his head. "You'll always be beautiful to me."

I let out a playful huff. "Even when I'm old and wrinkly?"

Kao's eyes meet mine for a moment, and before he can answer, screeching tires grab our attention.

Kao slams on the breaks, jerking the car to the right. "Shit." His right arm collides hard with my chest just before the noise of crushing metal fills my ears. It's followed by a loud bang and then something that sounds like rumbling thunder and lightning striking.

Pins and needles spread over my face from shock. "Kao!" I manage to let out a cry as the breath is knocked from my lungs. My body jerks forward, then to the side as our vehicle rolls before landing back on its tires. I'm slammed into the seat and then against the door. A burning pain spreads up my neck and face, and for a moment, everything blacks out.

'Starting 9-1-1 call. To cancel, press the 9-1-1 button on the mirror.'

The smell of burning rubber and oil fills my nose. Opening my eyes, I struggle to make sense of what's going on.

'Calling 9-1-1.'

Turning my head to the left, I let out a painful groan from the ache in my neck and head. I suck in a breath of air, and then my eyes focus on the driver's side.

I hear a dialing tone.

Shit.

It takes another couple of seconds before it begins to sink in that we were in an accident. "Kao," I croak, my voice sounding foreign to my own ears. My body begins to shiver uncontrollably.

"9-1-1, what's your emergency?" I hear an operator answer.

"A-accident," I struggle to say through the shock dazing me.

"Okay, we have your GPS coordinates. Emergency services have been dispatched. Are you hurt?"

My eyes are still widely glued to Kao. He doesn't move, and it makes panic flare through me like hot streaks of lava. "Kao!" When there's still no movement from him, I struggle with numb fingers to unclip my seatbelt. Once I'm free, I turn my body toward him and lean forward.

"Ma'am, are you hurt?"

My lips part and searing worry scorches my heart. "There's blood on the left side of his head."

"Did you say there's blood on your head?"

"N-no," I swallow hard on the bile pushing up my throat. "My boyfriend. There's blood on the side of his head."

"Help is on the way. Okay?"

I shake my head as my worry quickly morphs into ice-cold terror. "H-he's not moving," I stammer through the distress I'm feeling.

"Emergency services should be there any minute now," the operator assures me, but it does nothing to calm me.

Lifting my right arm, I press my fingers to Kao's pulse, and when I feel a beat, I let out a breath of relief. "He's alive."

"That's good. Ma'am, what's your name?"

"F-Fallon. Fallon Reyes." I move a little closer to Kao, my eyes frantically scanning over his body. Fear shudders

29

through me when I see more blood staining his shirt on his left side. "There's also blood on his left side."

"Where, Ma'am?"

"On his side, a couple of inches above his hip. There's more blood." I suck in a desperate breath. "Oh, God."

"Ma'am, help is on the way. Is anyone else hurt? Was another car involved?"

"I... I don't know."

"Okay, stay calm. Keep talking to me. What else do you see?"

Frantically, I glance around, taking in the crushed dashboard, the deflated airbags, the smoke rising from the front. My eyes snap back to Kao, and it's only when I see the blood again that the realization settles hard in my chest.

We were in an accident.

Kao's hurt.

"Hurry!" I cry. I bring a trembling hand to Kao's face but stop an inch from touching him, scared I'll hurt him more. "Kao? Baby?" A sob escapes my lips. "Kao?"

"You should hear the sirens any second now," the operator says.

Oh, God.

Please.

Let him be okay.

I lean a little closer, wanting so badly to hold him. "Kao?"

Emergency sirens fill the air, and moments later, my world spins into chaos when I'm pulled from the car. "No! Please. I want to stay with him."

The paramedic says something, but all I can hear are the different sirens from the emergency vehicles arriving at the scene. I'm placed on a stretcher, and my surroundings begin to blur as I'm rushed toward an ambulance.

No.

I need to stay with him.

When I get a glimpse of firemen moving around Kao's car, that's nothing but crumpled steel, horror washes all sense from me.

Noise fills the air, a mixture of urgent voices, sirens, and the firemen cutting through the metal of the vehicle, and then it's shut out as the doors of the ambulance are pulled closed.

My body feels numb, and I manage to blink a couple of times before darkness drags me away from the nightmare.

Feeling groggy, I open my eyes.

"Fallon? Honey?" I hear Mom's voice. Sluggishly, I move my eyes in her direction. Her face is strained with worry. "Oh, baby. You're going to be okay," she says, relief and exhaustion coating her words. "Thank God."

I open my mouth but first have to swallow hard on the dry lump stuck in my throat. "What happened?"

"You were in an accident." I feel Mom's tight hold on my hand.

Frowning, I sift through my jumbled memory until I latch onto one thing – Kao.

"Where's Kao? Is he okay?"

"He's still in surgery. Your dad went to check if there's any news." Mom brings a hand to my face and gently combs her fingers through my hair. "How do you feel?"

How do I feel?

Flashes from the accident ripple through me.

Kao smiling.

The deafening noise when we were hit.

The thick smell of oil.

The blood.

Kao not moving.

Agony builds in my chest until the pressure becomes too much, and it tears through me. "Kao," I manage to whimper as sobs wreck me.

Mom moves from the chair to sit on the side of the bed, and leaning over me, she begins to murmur, "Kao's strong. He'll pull through. A couple of days from now, this will all seem like a bad dream. Okay? You're both going to be fine."

I want so badly to believe her words.

I hear someone come into the private hospital room, and when Mom pulls back, my eyes collide with my father's.

He rushes forward to the other side of the bed, and I begin to struggle to sit up as more sobs wrack through me.

"Shh..." Daddy murmurs, and his movements are careful as he wraps his arms around me. "My beautiful girl, I'm here."

My body is stiff and sore, but I manage to wrap my arms around him and hold on for dear life as I cry my fears out in my father's strong hold.

"I just checked on Kao. He's in recovery. He's going to be okay. Leigh and Miss Sebastian assisted with the surgery. They're with him, and they'll make sure he gets the best care."

Miss Sebastian is an emergency nurse and Kao's godmother.

Mrs. West is Noah's mom and a cardiothoracic surgeon.

If they assisted with the surgery…

"Why did Mrs. West assist with the surgery? Did Kao…?"

Dad quickly shakes his head. "She's just here to make sure he gets the best possible care."

Remembering all the blood, I ask, "How badly is he hurt?"

"He had some internal bleeding, but they stopped it. There's a cut on his side that needed stitches."

When Dad pauses, the worry grows in my heart. "His head?"

"He has a hairline fracture. So far, everything looks promising. We have to wait for him to wake up."

I try to nod my head, but the brace and a tight pain in my neck keep me from moving. "My neck?" I whimper.

Daddy pulls back, and his eyes scan over my face. His gaze is gentle and reassuring as he says, "You have a concussion and whiplash. The doctor said you'll feel better in a couple of days."

I can see he's keeping something from me, and ask, "And?"

Dad brings a hand to my left cheek, and a heartbreaking look mixes with worry. It makes my heartbeat speed up, and I hold my breath, trying to steel myself for the blow to come.

"You have cuts on the side of your neck and on your right cheek. I've already found a plastic surgeon who can remove most of the scarring it might leave."

"Scarring?" I lift my hand, and when I feel the large dressing on the right side of my face, my heart shrinks into a fearful lump. "Is it bad?"

Again, Dad pauses, and it's all answer I need.

"Oh God," I gasp as my hand begins to tremble against the bandage. "It's bad, isn't it?"

"The plastic surgeon will fix it," Dad tries to reassure me. "Let's wait to hear what he says before we panic."

I nod even though it feels like my world has warped into an unrecognizable mess.

Scars.

I feel petrified, and... a foreign hopelessness makes my chest close up. The realization keeps washing over me like tidal waves, and an awful feeling numbs my insides with dread.

My fingers trace over the dressing until I reach the brace. Apprehension fills every part of me.

What am I going to do if...?

I try to breathe through the worry consuming me, and not able to deal with the fact that I might be scarred for life, I latch onto another fear.

Kao.

"Are you sure Kao will be okay?"

Dad nods. "The doctor is very optimistic for a full recovery."

And the other car?

"Do you know what happened?" I ask. "The other car? Are the people okay?"

Emotion flashes over Dad's face. "I haven't been to the accident scene yet, but the police said it should've been a head-on collision. Kao must've reacted quick enough because his side of the car took the brunt of the hit. The driver of the truck didn't make it. They think he fell asleep behind the wheel. There was another vehicle involved, but the driver is fine. She only has whiplash."

Someone died.

Even though it was that driver's fault, sadness still bleeds into my heart.

Then Dad's words sink in, and I ask, "It should've been a head-on collision?"

"Yes." Dad gives me a reassuring smile. "Luckily, it wasn't. Kao's a good driver."

But.

But...

I remember Kao jerking the steering wheel to the right as his arm pinned me to the seat.

He kept me safe.

He knew the truck was going to hit us, and he chose to keep me safe.

Oh God.

I told Kao to take that route. The accident wouldn't have happened if I hadn't...

I gasp for air as the thoughts shudder through me. "Daddy," I whimper, my emotions sky-rocketing.

Dad moves forward, wrapping me in a hug again. "You're both going to be okay."

I try to shake my head, but again I'm stopped by the brace and pain. "What if... what if..." I sob.

Daddy pulls back and framing my face with his hands, his eyes lock on mine. There's so much certainty in his gaze. "There are no what-ifs. Kao's surgery went well. He's stable. We found the best plastic surgeon for you. Everything will be fine." Dad lifts a hand and brushes some of my hair back. "We'll fix everything."

I've never doubted my parents. Not until today.

How will I live with the guilt of telling Kao which road to take?

How will I cope with facial scarring?

And Kao?

Oh, God, please let him be okay.

I don't know what I'd do if something were to happen to Kao. I'd never forgive myself.

Chapter 3

FALLON

It's been a day since the accident, and I've finally convinced Dad to get me a wheelchair so I can visit Kao.

Jase, Hunter, and Hana have hardly left my side while Noah, Jade, and Mila are with Kao.

They said he regained consciousness for a minute, but he was out of it. That was last night, and since then, he hasn't woken up again.

With every passing hour, worry consumes me. It feels like I've been thrust into the twilight zone. Nothing makes sense anymore. My emotions are all over the place, making me feel sick to my stomach.

"You should stay in bed," Hana mutters, not happy that I'm moving. "You have a concussion."

"I know," I mumble. Yes, I'm dizzy and nauseous, but I won't let anyone keep me from Kao a moment longer. "I just want to see him, then I'll come back."

Dad carefully lifts me from the bed and sets me down in the wheelchair.

"We can take her," Jase offers. "Then you and Aunt Layla can get something to eat."

"Thanks," Dad replies. "We won't be long."

Mom presses a kiss to the top of my head. "Don't stay out of bed for too long. Ten minutes then you're back. Okay?"

"I'll be fine," I mumble, tired of all the attention. I love my family and friends, but right now, all I can think of is Kao. I won't be able to rest until I've seen he's okay.

Jase pushes me out of the room and down the hallway. Luckily, due to our families' VIP status, we're both in private rooms, so we don't have to go far.

Hunter opens the door, and the moment Jase pushes me into the room, my eyes lock on the bed. "Stop."

Mr. Reed gets up from where he's sitting next to Kao, and the deep lines of worry etched on his face has my heart cracking.

I climb out of the wheelchair and slowly inch closer to the bed. There are machines hooked up to Kao, and the constant beeping doesn't offer me any comfort. There are red patches under his eyes and over his nose, and the left side of his face is black and blue, which makes the bandage around his head look stark white.

Reaching Kao, I swallow hard on the lump of emotion in my throat. I slowly inch forward until I'm able to wrap my fingers around his hand. Feeling the warmth from his skin, my eyes drift shut for a moment.

He's alive.

Gingerly, I lean over him, and I press my mouth to his cheek. Dark scruff has formed on his jawline from not shaving, and I feel the bristles against my lips.

"Sit, Fallon," Mr. Reed says. He takes hold of my arm and helps me into a chair he must've pulled closer.

My gaze darts up to Kao's father. "Is he okay? I heard he woke up?"

Kao got his blue eyes from his father, and looking into them, I feel the first semblance of comfort.

"Leigh says he'll be fine."

Leigh… Dr. West is a genius in her field. If she thinks Kao will be okay, then I'm hopeful he'll recover fully.

Noah comes into the room, and my gaze darts to him. "Is your mom sure he'll be fine?" I ask, needing to hear it from him.

Noah nods as he stops at the foot of the bed. His eyes drift over his best friend. "My mom assisted during the surgery. She said they repaired all the internal injuries. He has a hairline skull fracture, but the CT scan showed no damage to his brain. He's just out of it because his body needs to heal."

My gaze returns to Kao, and I take in every inch of his face. Seeing him so still is scary as hell, but I feel better after what Noah just said.

"Kao," I murmur, hoping he'll hear me. "It's Fallon. You need to wake up soon so I can see your eyes again."

I use the bed to pull myself back up, and leaning over Kao, I press a kiss to the corner of his mouth, then whisper, "Get better. Please."

I feel a hand on my back. "You need to get back to bed," Hana says.

I stare at Kao for a moment longer, wishing I didn't have to leave at all. "Please let me know if there's any change," I say as I straighten up. I glance from Mr. Reed to Noah. "Please."

"I will," Noah answers.

Jase helps me back into the wheelchair, and as he pushes me out of the room, it feels like a shadow falls around my shoulders. It's heavy and gloomy.

Kao's silent strength has always been there to keep me standing during hard times. Seeing him in such a fragile state… kills me.

KAO

Coming to, a pounding headache greets me. It's sharp, then dull, then intense again, like a heartbeat.

I'm nauseous, and there's a concentrated smell of sanitizer hanging around me like a thick cloud.

My body feels like it's been shredded to pieces, but through all the pain, one thought screams for attention. For some unknown reason, I need to make sure Fallon's okay.

I pry my eyes open, but I can't see anything.

My lips part and I suck in an agonizing breath before I'm able to murmur, "Fallon."

Is it night? What happened? I can't remember shit.

I move my right arm, trying to feel where I am, but I only find empty air and then a bed. Beeping from a machine close to me grabs my attention.

Am I in the hospital?

"You're awake," I hear Noah say, relief coating his words. "Finally. You had me worried."

"Noah?" Confused, I mutter, "Turn on a light."

He doesn't answer me, and I try to move into a sitting position. Pain sears through my stomach and chest, and it increases the pounding in my head.

"No, stay still." I feel his hands on my shoulders.

"What?" There's a flutter of panic in my chest. "Where am I? Why's it dark?" As I ask the questions, my mind fights the worry back, refusing to even think it.

"Shit," I hear Noah mutter. "Just stay still. I'm going to call the doctor."

Doctor?

I hear movement, then Noah says, "He just woke up." He continues to whisper something I can't make out.

I feel strong fingers wrap around mine. "Hey, my boy," Dad's voice quivers.

I shut my eyes tightly as the realization becomes impossible to ignore.

God. Please.

Was I in an accident?

My lashes lift slowly, anxiety building unbearably when I still can't see anything.

"Dad, what happened?" I whisper, my voice filled with apprehension. "I can't see anything."

I feel him move, guessing he's sitting on the bed next to me. His fingers skim the right side of my head. "Don't panic. You and Fallon were in a car accident. You took a blow to the head, and it's probably only temporary. Fallon's okay."

Temporary?

Fallon?

What the fuck happened?

I suck in a painful breath of air as everything spins into chaos inside me. Shutting my eyes, I try to focus on the headache, on the dull throb in my stomach and side.

I try to focus on anything but the stark reality that I can't see.

Dad presses a kiss to my temple, and I feel his lips quiver against my skin.

Fuck. No.

Please.

No.

The beeping begins to increase as my heartbeat speeds up.

"Everything's going to be okay," Dad murmurs. "I promise."

Slowly, I shake my head, and it feels like I'm losing grip with reality as the words fall over my lips, "I can't see."

I hear someone come into the room, and Dad pulls away from me.

"I thought there was no damage?" Dad grinds out, clearly upset, and it rips through me like a tornado.

"The CT scan showed nothing," a foreign voice answers. "The brain is complex. We'll do more tests now that Mr. Reed is awake."

A hand settles on my shoulder. "Mr. Reed, I'm Dr. Davis. Can you open your eyes for me?"

A part of me refuses to believe that I might be blind, and it keeps me from doing as the doctor asked.

"Kao?" Dad takes hold of my right hand. "Open your eyes."

I suck in a breath and hold it as I slowly open them.

Nothing.

God.

There's nothing.

Instantly, I'm thrown into a pit of despair as the breath rushes from me.

Dr. Davis does his checks. He talks with Dad, but I'm unable to take in anything. I hear more voices. Some panicked, others filled with devastation.

I remain still, blankly staring into a black chasm where no one can reach me. Time wraps into something incomprehensible.

Seconds. Minutes. Hours. They've all lost meaning.

Then a soft touch feathers over my left hand, and a familiar delicate scent chases the smell of sanitizer. *Fallon.* She presses a kiss to my cheek, and then I hear her whisper, "I missed you."

My eyes drift shut, and I desperately want to follow her voice to the light.

"Fallon." Her name is nothing more than a whisper, carrying the intensity of a prayer.

"I'm here." Her palm rests against my cheek, and she presses another kiss to my temple.

Through my despair, my worry for her still triumphs. "Are you okay?"

"I'm fine. Just whiplash and a little concussion. How do you feel?"

Her voice wraps me in a sheltered cocoon, where the truth of my situation can't follow me.

"Kao?" Her voice is gentle, and I can clearly hear her love for me. "How do you feel?"

Weird.

Scared.

Weak.

Lost.

My lips part. "Okay." I suck in an agonizing breath. "I'm okay."

I feel her move closer again. Her left cheek presses against mine, and her silky hair gets stuck on the scruff on my jaw. Then she whispers, "Thank you for waking up." Her breaths drift over my skin and ear. "Thank you for keeping me safe."

Fallon's okay.

But you lost your sight.

Fallon's okay. She's all that matters.

"We need to take Mr. Reed for a scan," a woman says.

Fallon begins to pull away, but with my right hand, I grab hold of her arm. "Wait." I pull her closer to me until I can feel her breath on my face again.

I try to lift my left arm, but the pain increases in my side, and it has me freezing for a moment. I breathe through it, then turning my head toward her, I ask, "You're okay, right?"

"Yeah," her answer flutters over my cheek.

I wish I could see for myself that she's not hurt.

I move my right hand up her back until I reach something that feels like foam and rubber instead of her neck.

"It's just a brace for the whiplash," she immediately answers.

My fingers skim over the foam until I feel her left ear, and then I move my hand into her hair and pull her closer. When her lips touch mine, I soak in the feel of them for a moment.

She's safe.

I cling to the relief as I let go of her.

"I'll wait for you to come back," Fallon says.

I open my eyes hoping – praying I'll see her beautiful face – but still, there's only darkness.

Shutting them again, I nod. "Later."

Chapter 4

FALLON

I stare at the covers on the bed as a nurse removes the neck brace.

Kao can't see anything.

The thought shudders through me for the hundredth time since Kao woke. They've done numerous scans and tests but haven't found the cause yet.

God, what if he's permanently blind?

I shove the thought away as soon as it pops into my head. They'll find out what's wrong and fix it. They have to.

Whatever the outcome, I'll be there for him.

I'll take care of him.

The nurse peels the bandage away from my skin on my neck. "The cuts are healing nicely. No infection."

"Good," I murmur. I haven't seen the gashes yet. I can't bring myself to look at the mess on my neck and face.

The nurse cleans the wounds and changes the dressings, and when she doesn't put the neck brace back on, I ask, "Am I done wearing the brace?" I freaking hope so. I'm tired of how scratchy it makes my skin feel.

"You'll need to wear it until your neck's better," she answers.

"Can I take a little break, though?"

"Just for a short while."

One small mercy, at least.

I let out a relieved sigh. "Thank you."

Dr. Menard, the plastic surgeon, will come to see me next Tuesday. I'm just hoping he'll be able to remove the scarring.

"It looks much better," Mom says, giving me a comforting smile.

Not wanting to talk about my injuries, I mutter, "I'm worried about Kao."

Mom reaches for my hand and gives it a squeeze. "I'm sure he'll be fine."

"I'm going to check on him." I slip off the bed.

Mom glances at her watch. "I'll head out then. I need to stop by the store, or your brother won't have anything for dinner."

"Forest's visiting tomorrow, right?" I ask.

"Yes, Aria and Carla will probably come with him."

The corner of my mouth lifts slightly because anything more will painfully pull at the cuts on my face.

I hug Mom before we leave the room. Walking down the hallway, I feel a little dizzy. The nurse said the sensation will come and go, but it will get better.

I push Kao's door open, and then I hear the doctor say, "Both corneas were damaged during the accident. It's probably from the force of the airbag deploying."

My gaze darts around the room, and I see Mr. and Mrs. Reed standing on one side of the bed. Noah and his mom, Mrs. West, is on the other side, with the attending doctor at the foot.

I slink into the room and softly shut the door behind me.

"Do you have corneas in the hospital's eye bank?" Mrs. West asks.

"I'll have to check, but if we don't, we can get a pair from another hospital," the doctor replies.

"Let me know. I can check with other hospitals as well," Mrs. West offers.

Kao lets out a bitter sounding chuckle, and everyone's eyes snap to him. His voice sounds deadly calm as he asks, "Can everyone leave?"

There's a moment's silence, then Mr. Reed places his hand on Kao's. "We're discussing the treatment."

Kao pulls his hand free, and there's no emotion on his face as he snaps, "I want to be alone. Just for a minute."

"It's all overwhelming, I know," the attending doctor sympathizes with him.

"Oh, do you?" Kao asks, his voice tight with anger. "I wasn't aware you're blind."

He doesn't get angry easily, so seeing him like this is unnerving.

"Let's give him a moment," Mrs. West says.

I stand to the side as they all file out of the room, then glance back at Kao. His eyes drift in my direction, and for a moment, it feels like he can actually see me.

My heart skips a hopeful beat, only to shatter once again when there's no recognition in his gaze.

"Should I leave as well?" I ask softly.

Please say no.

Emotion ripples over his face, then he asks, "Has everyone left?"

"Yeah, It's just me." I walk a little closer. "And you."

Kao lifts his right hand, reaching in my direction, and it makes me dart forward. I take hold of him and ask, "Want to talk about it?"

He shuts his eyes and shakes his head, letting out an exhausted sigh. "I just... it's too fast, too much. I need to think."

"My hermit," I tease as I sit down on the side of the bed. "You've never liked a lot of people hovering around you."

The corner of his mouth lifts. It's only for a second before the hard lines are back. I lift a hand to his face, and when my fingers touch his jaw, he jerks.

I pause, and it makes him whisper, "Sorry."

He lifts his left hand and places it over mine, pressing my palm to his jaw.

"Open your eyes," I whisper.

Kao shakes his head, a pained look tightening his features.

"Please."

His lashes slowly lift, and I get to see the clear blue I love so much.

"They say they can do a cornea transplant," he murmurs.

"I heard. That's good, right?"

It looks like he's caught in a daydream, his eyes not moving at all.

"Yeah," he mutters, but there's no conviction in the single word.

I swallow hard as a lump threatens to push up my throat. I wish I had the power to heal him.

"If I focus hard, I can see a million tiny lights… and streaks," he admits, his voice hoarse with hopelessness. "It's like I just closed my eyes."

I lean closer. "You'll see again. It's not permanent."

His right hand takes hold of my waist, and he pulls me against him. I wrap my arms around his neck, and we hug for a moment, then Kao turns his face toward me. "What's on your neck and face?"

I pull back a little, instantly feeling self-conscious.

We'll really be beauty and the beast now.

"Just bandages," I murmur.

Kao pushes me further back, and his left hand bumps into my arm before moving up to my neck. When his fingers brush over the dressing, a frown forms between his eyes.

"You said you didn't get hurt?"

"It's nothing," I lie to put him at ease. "Just a couple of cuts. My dad got a plastic surgeon. I'm meeting with him on Tuesday." I swallow hard as apprehension fills my chest. "It's no big deal."

Kao's hand falls to his lap, and for the longest seconds, he doesn't move. His voice sounds pained when he finally says, "Cuts? Surgery?" He begins to shake his head. "You got hurt."

I reach for his hand, but the moment I touch him, he jerks his hand away. My heart begins to beat heavily. I've never seen Kao react this way. Not even when Mila was attacked.

Oh, God. He's not going to want me anymore.

"It's nothing," I lie again, hoping to set him at ease. Maybe I'm lucky, and the surgeon can remove all of the scarring before Kao has his sight back. "Don't worry about it."

"You got hurt," he bites the words out.

"Yeah, but it's not serious," I keep lying.

My gaze is locked on his face, and I watch as a pained expression darkens his features… and then he shuts his eyes.

"Leave," he grinds out between clenched teeth.

Shock shudders through me, and my lips part on a gasp, "What?"

Kao's breathing speeds up, and then he shouts, "Leave, Fallon!"

Recoiling, I gasp, "Kao?" My heart is kicking against my ribs. I can't believe he's treating me so harshly. Kao was never a vain person. Having him react so strongly because of the cuts has my heart shattering into a million pieces.

"Get out," he barks.

I flinch away and getting up from his bed, the broken pieces of my heart rattle in my chest.

I watch his hands clench tightly into fists, and then Kao shouts, "Stop staring and get the fuck out!"

My hand flies to my mouth and shocked by his extreme behavior, I rush toward the door.

Before I can open it, Noah comes in. "What's going on?"

"He found out about the cuts on my face and neck." I shake my head, still shocked by Kao's reaction.

"Noah?" Kao snaps.

Noah gives me a worried look, then he answers, "Yeah, I'm here."

"Make sure she leaves," he orders.

"Go," Noah whispers, and lifting his hand, he gives my arm a squeeze. "I'm sure he's just wound tight from everything that's happened. Don't worry."

I nod and glance back at Kao before I step out of the room.

Standing in the hallway, I try to make sense of what just happened. Kao's never talked to me like that. He's never raised his voice.

Until I visited with Kao, I still felt hopeful that the plastic surgeon would be able to fix me. But now that I've seen Kao's anger and… revulsion? I'm not sure anything can repair the damage done.

KAO

Fallon got hurt.

Because of me.

Cuts?

Seriously? Fallon talked about it as if it was nothing. I felt the bandages. It covered the whole right side of her neck and face.

Just fucking cuts?

She'll have to go for surgery. That means more pain.

It's no big deal?

Is she fucking kidding me?

Noah lets out a sigh, and it has me snapping, "Leave!"

"Is that your new favorite word?" he asks, sounding bored as fuck.

Frowning, I turn my head in his direction. "Don't start with me," I warn him.

"I'm not starting anything. You have the losing your shit part all handled." The sarcastic tone in his voice only makes me angrier.

"Just get out," I grind the words through clenched teeth. Getting into a fight with Noah is the last thing I have strength for.

"Nope," he taunts me. He even let's the fucking 'p' pop.

I sit still for a moment, trying to breathe through the anger that's threatening to tear a gaping hole through everything I know. Everything I ever believed.

I thought Fallon and I were one of a kind. I thought we shared something unbreakable. I was so careful with her. I wanted everything to be perfect for her.

But all it took was me fucking things up. One moment and I almost killed her.

God.

I could've killed Fallon.

My breathing speeds up, and unable to sit still, I push through the pain in my side and climb off the bed.

"You need the restroom?" Noah asks.

I feel his hand on my arm as I stare into the dark abyss that's become my new normal.

Only, it's far from normal.

It's a fucking nightmare.

I push Noah away from me. "Get out!"

"Kao," he snaps, my name filled with warning. "I get you're upset, but you need to calm down."

"Calm down?" I growl.

Stupidly, I try to glance around the room. It's reflexes like this that trip me. Besides the dark pit of black ink, that's a constant reminder, habits make it so much worse.

I blindly swing at anything... something, and the back of my hand connects with the glass of water that was next to the bed. I hear it shatter, and it drives me to keep going. I need to sow destruction. I need to let out the anger... the despair... the fucking guilt.

I almost killed Fallon.

I hurt her.

I fucking scarred the woman I love.

Arms come around me, and I instantly know they belong to my father. He pins me to his chest.

One.

Two.

Three.

I suck in a desperate breath and then let out a shout, hoping it will rid me of the chaos.

"I've got you," Dad says, and he pulls me down to the floor. I let my body slump against his as another cry tears through me.

I was supposed to keep her safe.

I... I... I fucked everything up.

I fucking deserve to be blind.

At least then I won't have to see the damage I've done. I won't have to face the destruction I've caused.

Dad's arms tighten around me. "Shhh... I'm here."

I shake my head because not even that's enough any longer. This is something my father can't fix for me.

The worst part? I can't even remember the accident. I can't recall the moment my life lost all meaning.

My body shakes in my father's hold as the agony of what I've done to Fallon rips my soul to shreds.

Once again, time warps into nothing but bitterness and crippling guilt.

I don't know how long Dad holds me, his words of reassurance bouncing off the hellish chaos that's enveloped me. Somehow, I manage to calm down. But it feels empty, like the silence when you're caught in the eye of a storm, waiting for the second half to hit.

"They've scheduled the transplant for Monday," Dad reminds me. "You'll get your vision back."

I shake my head as I let Dad help me to my feet. I bump against the side of the bed before I carefully sit down on it.

The doctor said there's a ten percent chance the transplant won't work. Even if it's a success, so much can still go wrong. I'll probably never get my full vision back.

And honestly... I don't have the guts to face what I've done to Fallon.

"No." The word falls hard in the room.

"No?" Dad asks. "For what?"

"I won't go through with the transplant."

This black hole will be my prison for what I've done to her.

Chapter 5

FALLON

Noah burst into my room, a thunderous expression etched on his face. "Can you come talk to Kao?"

I'm still a mess from Kao's reaction to my injuries and haven't even started to process anything. Somehow, I manage to push the covers off me. "Did something happen?" I ask, my voice hoarse from the raw heartache.

Noah frustratingly thrusts a hand through his hair. "He's losing his shit and refusing the transplant."

"What?" I gasp. I climb off the bed, and with my own pain shoved to the side, I rush out of the room. My thoughts are instantly consumed with worry for Kao. "That's insane!"

"Yeah. He won't even listen to Uncle Marcus. I thought maybe you can get through to him."

We hurry to the room, and as I near the door, I hear Kao shout, "I've made up my mind!"

"I won't let you do this to yourself," Mr. Reed hollers just as I step inside. "You will go through with the transplant."

"Dad," Kao yells, "Drop it!"

Mr. Reed's breaths race over his lips, his face torn between frustration and heartbreak.

Kao, on the other hand, looks murderous. I've never seen that expression on his face before, and it makes a shiver ripple through me.

I swallow hard before I walk closer. "Kao?"

His head snaps in my direction, and pain flits over his features before the granite expression returns. Then he growls, "What are you doing here?"

"I called her," Noah admits. "Someone needs to talk some sense into your stubborn ass."

"Can everyone just fucking leave me alone?" Kao snaps.

I flinch from all the anger coming off him, and my heart begins to beat heavily in my chest.

"Can you stop throwing a fucking tantrum for one minute?" Noah barks at Kao. "For fucks sake, you're impossible!"

I let out a gasp when Kao stands up from where he was sitting on the side of the bed. His movements are filled with rage, but my heart splits right down the middle when I watch him reach his hands out to feel where he's going.

I can't move a muscle as Kao comes toward me. His hand connects with my arm, and it makes him freeze.

I begin to reach for him, but then he shuts his eyes, and with his voice low, he hisses, "Out of my way."

Ignoring him, I step forward and wrap my arms around his waist. I press my left cheek to his chest and say, "I won't. You'd be there for me, so let me help."

His hands settle on my shoulders, and he pauses. I feel his breath stir my hair, but then he pushes me back. Letting out a bitter sounding chuckle, he says, "You're scarred." He shakes his head, and moving me to the side, he lets go of me. "Nothing's going to change that." Another bitter chuckle grates against my ears.

"Kao!" Mr. Reed snaps.

"What the fuck?" Noah growls.

Devasted, I can only stare at Kao. The fact that he's disgusted with me rips my broken heart clean from my chest.

A foreign emotion creeps into the empty space left in my rib cage. I've always been able to hug and touch Kao. Whenever I wanted to. He was my person. My love. Not being able to comfort him is the worst torture. But having

65

him being repulsed by me – makes it feel like a gaping gorge is being torn open between us.

Everything I ever thought I knew about Kao Reed is stripped from my memory until I'm staring at a stranger.

How could I be so wrong about him? I thought he was kind, loyal, and strong.

I was wrong.

This stranger is cruel. My Kao wouldn't care about the scars. He'd tell me they don't matter.

Sucking in a painful breath, I close my eyes as I turn around and start to walk away from him.

"Fallon," Mr. Reed calls after me.

I stop outside in the hallway, and it's hard to meet Mr. Reed's blue eyes.

"I'm so sorry," he apologizes for his son's behavior.

It takes all my strength to fight back the threatening tears, and I manage to smile, welcoming the pain in my cheek. "Don't worry. Kao's going through a lot."

Mr. Reed reaches for my arm and gives it a squeeze. "And he's stubborn. Please, give him time."

I nod, my smile not wavering. "Of course."

"Thank you."

I watch Mr. Reed hurry back inside, and feeling like half a woman, I dazedly walk to my room. Once inside, I shut the door behind me, and then my lips part as I let the devastation wreak havoc through me. I gasp for air and clutch at my shirt over my heart.

Oh, God. Make it stop. It hurts too much.

A sob tears through my throat, making my neck cramp.

It feels like Kao died in the accident.

We didn't survive.

The door slams into my back, and I stagger forward. Jase comes in, and the second his eyes land on me, he darts forward. His arms wrap around me, and I cling to my cousin, desperate for him to make the pain go away.

"I'm here," he murmurs while rubbing my back. "It's going to be okay."

I shake my head and pull away. Using the back of my hand, I wipe the tears from my left cheek. "It won't. He hates me. He's… he's disgusted with the scars."

"What the fuck?" Jase's eyebrows knit angrily together. "Who?"

Just remembering what Kao said has my face crumbling again as I gasp, "Kao." I move back into Jase's arms. "He hates me."

"Shh." Jase's arms tighten around me. "Kao's in shock. I'm sure he didn't mean it."

Jase's words offer me no comfort. It was too easy for Kao to change. One moment he wanted a relationship with me, and the next, I'm nothing to him?

The question only deepens the heartache, and it makes me feel like I'll never be whole again.

KAO

Dad and Noah are pissed off with me. Actually, that's an understatement. But I couldn't care less. I can't face what I've done to Fallon, and they won't understand even if I tried to explain.

My emotions keep alternating between rage and guilt, both equally debilitating. It feels as if I'm at war with myself.

I want to hold Fallon and assure her everything will be okay, but how can I? Nothing will ever be okay again.

Nothing will change the fact that I almost killed her. She's better off keeping her distance from me, and if I have to be an asshole to make her stay away, then so be it. I'd rather lose her love and respect than having to face a world she's not in because I killed her.

Just thinking about the cuts on her face and neck and the surgery she'll have to face makes it feel like my soul weighs a ton from the regret bearing down on me.

I wish I could go back and change things. I'd never ask Fallon out to dinner. I'd give up on my dream of being with her. Anything to ensure her safety.

But it's too late.

Now, there's nothing. Nothing but fucking darkness and emptiness.

"Baby?" I hear Mom, and when her hand brushes over my cheek, it makes everything worse instead of better.

Mom raised me to be a gentleman. To always protect the women in my life.

I failed to protect the most important one.

I hear the swishing of fabric. "I've brought you a couple of things." She places something in my hand. "This is an iPad. I had the settings adjusted, so if you touch the screen, it will tell you where you're at." Mom moves my hand until my finger bumps against the screen.

'Music. Double-tap to open,' a voice sounds up.

You've got to be fucking kidding me. I know Mom means well, but this is just another reminder that I'm blind as fuck.

Even though my world has gone to shit, I still force a smile to my face and mutter, "Thanks, Mom."

"Remember, the flap opens to the left. That way, you'll know you have it the right side up."

I nod and then hear the rustling of papers.

"I brought you snacks and placed them in the drawer," Mom explains. "Think of it as a treasure hunt. They're all your favorites, though."

"Yeah? You're not going to try and sneak in some veggies?" I tease her.

"Damn, I should've thought of that. I'll sneak some in next time," Mom chuckles.

When her hand closes over mine, I ask, "Aren't you going to lay into me, as well?"

"No." Her fingers squeeze mine. "Right now, I'm just going to love and support my son. We'll deal with the transplant when you feel better."

Silence fills the room, and my mother's soothing presence wraps like a protective cloak around me.

"I hurt Fallon," I murmur.

"It was an accident," Mom replies, her tone soft.

"I could've killed her."

"Baby," Mom breathes. "It wasn't your fault."

"I should've protected her," I argue.

"You did." Mom's hand brushes up and down my forearm, and when I shake my head, she continues, "You took the full brunt of the truck hitting your car to keep Fallon safe."

"Not safe enough," I grumble. "She's scarred."

"Her parents got the best plastic surgeon. I'm sure he'll be able to remove all the scarring."

Just thinking about Fallon going in for surgery makes what's left of my heart shrivel until it feels like it will fade to nothing any second. I can't bear the thought of her having to endure more pain.

I just shake my head, not wanting to talk about Fallon anymore. It's too hard.

God, why did I ask her out for dinner? Why did this have to happen?

I shut my eyes against the hopelessness and despair.

Mom lets out a breath, and I can feel her searching for the right words to say.

"It's okay, Mom," I say to put her at ease. "I just need some time."

I can't tell what the time is as I blink into the dark nothingness around me.

I hear Noah's breaths, where he's asleep on the couch in my hospital room.

I suck in a suffocating breath. This hell is killing me. All I can do is just fucking lie here while it feels like I'm wasting away.

I can't change anything. I can't go to Fallon. I can't see. I fucking... can't.

Sitting up, I angrily shove the covers away from me. I throw my legs over the side of the bed and grip the mattress hard.

I hurt Fallon. She's scarred because of me.

I fucking hate myself.

An enraged growl builds in my chest, and I push off the bed.

It feels like I'm going insane. The guilt keeps pounding relentlessly against my heart that already feels like nothing but a worthless piece of shit.

The ever-present darkness makes everything so much worse. There's nothing to distract myself with. Only the endless night and the constant reminder of what I've done.

I can't be with Fallon. I won't be able to finish my studies. It's like someone pressed delete on my life.

What am I going to do?

Fuck.

What's left to live for?

Anger, frustration, and guilt swirl in me, not giving me a second's reprieve.

I begin to stumble in the direction of the door, or where I think it will be. Every step makes my heartbeat speed up.

I'm fucking useless now.

I hear my breaths as they burst over my lips. My skin prickles, and bringing my arms up, my hands keep touching empty air until I knock into something hard. It feels like the wall, and I move my hands over it until I finally reach the door.

I have to get out of here. I'm fucking losing my mind.

I manage to open the door and stick close to the wall as I step out of the room.

The darkness stretches endlessly around me. It strips me of my independence and makes me... blind.

Pressure builds in my chest, and I begin to breathe faster, but it doesn't feel like any of the air is getting to my lungs.

With my back plastered against the wall, I bleakly try to glance around me.

The blow hits again.

The pressure builds more.

Bringing my hands up, I grip fistfuls of my hair as I try to breathe faster.

I feel paralyzed. Lost. Dead.

I'm alone in the dark. So fucking alone.

My body jerks as tears threaten to fall, and I bring my hands down to cover my face.

"Kao?" I hear Noah's voice.

It's become so unbearable, I instantly turn toward the sound of his voice and reach out. Noah takes hold of my arm and pulls me back into the room. I hear the door shut, and then his arms grip me tightly. I grab hold of Noah, knowing I'll fade to nothing without him.

An agonizing gasp escapes me, and I shake my head, unable to accept that my life has ended.

I'm only twenty-three.

This can't be it. This can't be my future.

This can't be all that's left of my life.

"We're going to fix everything," Noah murmurs.

I shake my head again. "She's scarred," I whisper. "I'm blind." I tighten my hold on Noah as the guilt and despair rip through me once more.

"One thing at a time. Go for the surgery. Let's get your vision back," Noah tries to convince me.

"Not now," I grind the words out, unable to cope. "I can't handle fighting with you now."

Noah's arms become steel bands as he keeps me standing. "Okay," he murmurs. "I've got you. We'll get through this."

Nothing he says helps to ease the fear and hopelessness. Shutting my eyes, everything I was, everything I lived for, is stripped from me.

Something dies inside me, and I begin to pull back, but Noah grips me tighter and growls, "Don't you fucking dare push me away. I won't let you. You're my fucking brother, and I'll take all your shit, but I won't let you shut me out."

Feeling numb, I stand in his arms as I whisper, "Noah." It feels like I'm shutting down. "There's... nothing." It feels like the darkness is swallowing me. "Just nothing."

Chapter 6

FALLON

The past three days have been the hardest I've ever had to endure. The shock of Kao's reaction to my injuries and him refusing the cornea transplant still shudders through me.

I can't make any sense of what happened.

Unable to stay away from him, I stand outside his room. I'm trying to build up enough courage to go inside.

I want to see him before I go back to Trinity. My parents wanted me to go home, but I don't want to fall behind with my studies. Also, staying close to my friends helps ease the heartache a little.

I take a fortifying breath and then push the door open. When I walk into the room, Noah's eyes dart to me from where he's sitting next to Kao's bed.

Noah looks so tired.

I move closer, and my gaze shifts to Kao.

"He's sleeping," Noah whispers. "We had a rough night."

Instantly a lump forms in my throat. I stop on the other side of the bed, and my eyes slowly caress every inch of Kao. Staring at his beautiful face, the sting from the cruel words lessen.

For a deceitful moment, it almost feels normal. Like Kao and I haven't been torn apart.

Not able to stop myself, I lean over him, and I press my lips to his cheek. I take a deep breath of his scent.

God, I love him so much. Please let him come back to me.

All I want to do is lie down beside him and hold him until we're both healed. I want to pretend there isn't a gaping hole between us.

Instead, I have to force myself to pull back.

When I see the hard lines around his mouth, I know he's awake. The relaxed look is gone and replaced with anger.

I shake my head, not able to accept what's happening between Kao and me.

We are stronger than this. We were inseparable. We love each other.

Don't we?

I've never actually said the words to Kao, but I'm sure he knows how I feel about him. There's never been anyone but him.

"Kao," I whisper, the hopelessness I feel shimmering in my voice, "how do you feel?"

His eyes slowly open, and all the warmth I used to bathe in is gone and replaced with an icy expression. "I'd feel a hell of a lot better if you'd leave."

His words hit like a physical blow, and I stumble a step backward.

Noah gets up and walking to me, he comes to place an arm around my waist. "Come, Fallon." His voice is the opposite of Kao's, filled with compassion.

I let Noah pull me out of the room, trapped in a world of confusion and heartache.

Noah walks me back to my room before he says, "Just give him time."

I shake my head as I face Kao's best friend. "Will that really help? It's like he's a stranger."

Noah's features soften as he moves his hand to my shoulder, giving it a squeeze. "He's angry because you got hurt."

My eyes lock on Noah's. "It doesn't feel like it. I heard the revulsion in his voice."

"Because of what happened," Noah argues. "Kao blames himself."

"Did he tell you that?" I ask, hopeful that it could really be the reason.

Maybe it's not because he's repulsed by me?

Noah gives my shoulder another squeeze. "He didn't have to tell me. I know him better than anyone. I'm sure that's the reason. As soon as the shock wears off and he gets the transplant, he'll be back to normal."

My eyes widen as more hope pours into me. "Did he agree to the surgery?"

Frustration flits over Noah's face, giving me my answer before he mutters, "Not yet. I'm working on changing his mind."

I shake my head, helplessness dimming the little hope I had. "I don't understand why he won't have the transplant."

"He's just angry right now," Noah explains.

"I wish he'd let me be there for him," I admit.

"Don't take it personally, Fallon." Noah lets out a tired sigh. "He's trying to push me away as well."

My hermit.

The thought makes the corner of my mouth lift slightly.

"Are you going back to campus today?" Noah asks.

79

I nod. "Yeah, Hunter and Hana are coming to get me. They should be here soon."

"I'll see you back at the dorm then."

Noah begins to walk to the door, and it has me saying, "Noah." He glances at me from over his shoulder. "Thank you."

The corners of his mouth lift slightly before he leaves my room.

To keep busy, I make sure I've packed everything. Knowing I'm going back to Trinity, I walk to the bathroom as I untie my hair. While I brush it, so half is hanging over the right side of my face, my eyes go over the bandages.

I still haven't seen what the cuts look like. The doctor said I have to keep the dressings on until the stitches come out. I'm allowed to shower and clean the cuts daily.

The thought of having to take care of the wounds myself makes my chest fill with apprehension.

Movement from the room has me sucking in a deep breath before I walk out of the bathroom to greet Hunter and Hana.

"Are you ready?" Hunter asks, his eyes falling on the bag next to the bed.

"Yeah."

Hana's gaze locks on me, and then worry makes her frown. "Did something happen?"

"I went to see Kao," I mutter. "He wasn't too happy about it."

Hunter lets out a deep breath. "Yeah, he's distant with all of us."

I pick up my sweater from the bed and shrug it on. "Noah said Kao's angry and even trying to push him away."

"I'm sure once he gets the surgery and can see again, he'll be back to his usual self," Hana says.

Hunter grabs my overnight bag. "Yeah, honestly, I'd be out of my mind if I were blind. We have to put ourselves in his shoes."

"I just wish he'd let me help him," I say as we walk out into the hallway. Nearing Kao's room, my pace slows, and I'm overwhelmed with the urge to go to him.

I hate leaving him here.

"Give me a second," I say, and then I push the door open and steeling myself for Kao's anger, I walk to the side of his bed and leaning over him, I press a kiss to his cheek. Straightening up, I say, "I'm going home, but I'll come to visit. Noah can call me if you need me to bring anything for you."

"Don't bother," Kao says, the words sounding tight.

Ignoring Kao, I glance at Noah. "Are you staying the whole day?"

Noah gives me a grin. "Yeah."

"Want me to bring you something to eat tonight?"

"A burger would be awesome."

"Should've known he won't miss out on a chance for junk food," Hunter jokes.

I even manage to smile a little. "With bacon and cheese?"

"Extra cheese."

I glance at Kao again. "Get some rest, Kao." It's on the tip of my tongue to tell him I love him, but I swallow the words back and hurry out of the room.

"Hope you feel better soon," I hear Hana tell Kao before she joins me out in the hallway.

KAO

"I'll come by with Jade a little later," Hunter says.

Fuck, is the whole crowd here?

After a minute, Noah grumbles, "You can stop scowling. They're all gone."

I let out a tired breath and shut my eyes.

"It's bullshit, though," he keeps muttering. "I totally get you're angry and frustrated, but you're treating your family and friends like shit." I hear a chair creak. "This has to stop. Go for the fucking surgery and put us all out of our misery."

I clench my jaw until I hear a door shut. "Noah?" I only get silence as an answer and figure he probably left.

Tired of lying down, I shift into a sitting position. A weird sensation ripples over me as if I'm not alone. I turn my face to the right, and a frown starts to form. "Who's there?"

I can feel the air move. "It's me," Jase answers.

Fuck.

"Why won't you go for the surgery?"

I suck in another breath and shake my head. I seriously don't have the strength to take on Jase. The second he finds out I'm refusing because I don't want to see what I did to Fallon, he'll lose his shit.

"There's no guarantee it will work," I go with the safer option. It's not a lie. There's no guarantee I'll ever see again.

Just thinking about it makes the air rip from my lungs as the blow hits for what feels like the millionth time.

"So? It's worth the risk. It's not like you can get anymore blind than you already are." His words are harsh and cold, sending a shiver of anger rushing through me.

"For fuck sakes," I grind the words out. "Just leave."

Jase lets out a chuckle that sounds more like a warning. "And leave you to wallow in self-pity? Not a chance in hell." I can feel him move closer. "Look, I understand it's hard as fuck. It sucks that it happened, but you can't let one accident define your whole life."

"Fuck, Jase. Seriously?" I snap. "How the fuck do you understand? I don't have much of a choice. This is my fucking life now."

"It doesn't have to be," he argues. "Go for the surgery."

I shake my head again as I let out a frustrated huff. "Leave it be."

There's a moment's silence, then Jase says, "I never took you for the kind to just give up."

"Whatever," I mumble, tired of having the same fight with every family member and friend coming through the fucking door.

"Yeah," Jase mutters. "Whatever." He moves like a damn ninja because I can't hear shit until the door opens.

"You're breaking Mila and Fallon's hearts. Keep going on this road of self-destruction, and I'll be beating the shit out of you."

I hear the door shut and scowl into the darkness. It's easy for Jase to talk. He's not the one who hurt Fallon. He isn't blind.

I squeeze my eyes tightly shut.

Fuck. I'm going to lose everyone.

I hear the door again and start to shake my head, beyond frustrated and angry. "Can everyone just leave me alone!"

"Looks like he's in a piss poor mood," I hear Uncle Jax.

My body instantly tenses. Uncle Jax is the one person who might see through all of my bullshit. He dealt with my dad years ago when he almost died.

"You can say that again," Dad mutters.

Fuck.

Both of them?

"Are you ganging up on me now?" I let out an empty sounding chuckle.

I feel them take a seat on either side at the foot of the bed, then Uncle Jax replies, "We're here because we care."

When I keep quiet, Dad says, "I wasn't blind, but I'm pretty sure I know what you're going through."

I knew it was only a matter of time before we had this talk. Truth be told, I dreaded it. Dad's been through his own hell, and I won't be able to turn a deaf ear. Not when it comes to my father being so close to dying. Just thinking about it sends a shudder down my spine.

"I know how hopeless and frustrated you feel. I know how angry you are." Dad's words make emotion build in my chest. "I also know how alone you feel."

I shut my eyes against the wave of despair.

"But you're not alone," Uncle Jax says. "You have so many people who love you."

I nod, and lifting my head, I whisper, "I know."

"Why won't you get the transplant?" Uncle Jax asks.

Even though I know the reason won't hold much ground with them, I answer, "There's a chance it won't work."

"Ten percent, Kao," Dad pleads. "There's a ninety percent chance of you seeing again. Fuck, I didn't even have a five percent chance of surviving."

Bringing my right arm up, I rub a hand over my face. "I know, Dad."

Fallon.

I can't bear to see what I did to her.

"What's the real reason?" Uncle Jax asks.

I swear he has a built-in bullshit detector.

I shake my head, not willing to admit my guilt to them. I'm too fucking ashamed.

"Fine," Uncle Jax mutters. "What do you plan on doing with your life if you're so fucking intent on not ever seeing again?"

Nothing. Just fucking nothing.

My silence makes Dad grab hold of my shoulders. "Stop this shit, Kao." His breaths sound angry, and I can't blame him. I can't blame any of them for losing their patience with me. "Christ! You still have your whole life ahead of you. Don't fuck it up like this."

Needing them to back off, I lie, "I'll think about it. Okay? I just… I need time to process everything."

Dad pulls me into a hug, and his voice is raw by my ear, "Please, Kao. If not for yourself, do it for me."

When Dad pulls back, I turn my head in his direction. "Give me a week."

By then, I should be able to discharge myself and lock my pathetic ass in a hotel room.

"Just one week?" Dad asks. The hopeful tone in his voice kills what's left of my spirit.

"Yeah."

Chapter 7

FALLON

Walking into the suite I share with my friends, it feels empty even though Hana and Hunter are with me.

"Want me to order you something for lunch?" Hunter asks.

The corner of my mouth lifts slightly. I'm so thankful I have such caring friends. "A salmon salad would be nice."

"On it," Hunter grins at me while pulling his phone out of his pocket so he can call the order into the restaurant.

"Is Fallon home?" I hear Jade call before she and Mila come rushing down the hallway. The moment they see me, Jade lets out a happy shriek and then wraps me up in a huge hug. "It's so good to have you back."

When Jade pulls away and Mila moves closer, wrapping her arms around me, emotion pushes up my throat. We haven't hugged much since she was attacked, so this means a lot to me.

Mila pulls back and asks, "How do you feel?"

"Better." The left corner of my mouth lifts a little.

There's a knock at the door, and Hunter goes to open. He lets out a bark of laughter, and when my mom and Aunt Kingsley come in, I understand why.

A chuckle bubbles over my lips when I see the arrangement of chocolate flowers in Aunt Kingsley's arms.

They both kiss my left cheek, then Aunt Kingsley holds the gift out to me. "I figured you could do with some comfort food, and seeing as you're allergic to flowers, I thought this would be a good replacement for the real thing."

"Thank you so much," I grin at my aunt. Taking the basket from her, I go to set it down on the kitchen counter.

Mom comes to place a hand on my lower back. "Did you just get back?"

"Yeah," I nod as I turn to her. "We stopped by Kao's room before leaving."

Mom's eyes settle on the bandages. "Did they clean the cuts before you checked out of the hospital?"

I nod. "I only have to clean them again tomorrow morning."

"I'll come over and help."

I give Mom a thankful smile. "Thanks."

"Have you all had lunch?" Aunt Kingsley asks.

"Not yet," Hunter answers his mom. "I was just about to order in for Fallon."

Aunt Kingsley's gaze turns to me. "You don't want to go to the restaurant?"

I shake my head, not yet ready to mingle with the other students.

"Want to give me all the orders, and I'll call the restaurant?" Hunter asks.

While they're all busy, I pick up my overnight bag and walk to my room. I stop at my door, and my gaze goes to Kao's bedroom. Setting the bag down, I walk the short distance, and once I'm inside, I shut his door behind me.

His familiar scent hangs in the air, and I take a deep breath. My eyes scan over his desk where his laptop lies.

My heart squeezes into a tiny lump, and when I see the shirt he wore to classes on Wednesday lying on the side of his bed, I walk closer. Picking it up, I press it to my face, and when I smell him, tears push up my throat.

God, I miss you, Kao.

I still can't believe how horribly everything has changed over the past three days.

I set the dirty shirt back on the bed and walking to Kao's closet, my hand brushes over all of his shirts before I pull one out. I walk to the bathroom, and picking up his aftershave bottle, I squirt some onto the fabric and then take it with me.

At least, this way, it will feel like he's still close by.

―――――――――――――

It's been a long day with family and friends all taking turns to check on me.

After dressing in a clean pair of jeans and a t-shirt, I make sure my hair covers the dressings on my face and neck before I walk out of my room.

When I get to the kitchen to grab Noah's burger, which was delivered a couple of minutes ago, Jase and Mila come into the suite. They must've gone for dinner.

Jase's gaze falls on my car keys as I pick them up. "Where are you going?"

"To visit Kao." I begin to walk toward them.

"I'll take you," Jase says. Not waiting for my answer, he takes my car keys from me and throws them back in the bowl on the counter.

Knowing it won't help to argue with him, I let it go. We all file out of the suite. If I'm honest with myself, I'm glad they're coming along. Maybe then Kao won't be as angry. He has a soft spot for Mila, especially after the attack.

Stepping into the elevator, I shake my head at myself. It sucks that I'm using my friends to hide behind. It's just... I can't handle much more. Kao's rage is something I'll never get used to.

Once we're in Jase's car, I stare out of the window at the landscape passing by us.

"How are you holding up?" Jase asks.

"I'm good."

"Don't lie to me, Fallon," he murmurs.

My eyes meet Jase's in the rearview mirror. He's always been so damn perceptive, you can't hide anything from him.

My shoulders slump as I suck in a deep breath. "I'll be okay. It's just hard right now," I admit the truth.

"I saw Kao earlier," Jase says.

"Yeah? How was he?"

"Angry."

Yeah, that about sums it up.

"I just wish he'd go for the surgery," Mila voices her hope.

"I don't understand why he won't," I admit.

"I think he's scared it might not be a success. He doesn't want to get his hopes up," Jase gives his opinion.

"But it's worth the chance," I argue.

Jase lets out a sigh as he pulls into the hospital's parking area. "I told him that."

We all climb out, and Jase walks between Mila and me. We're quiet until we reach the VIP floor.

Jase places his hand on my back. "Whatever happens, I'm here."

I give him a grateful smile before I push open the door.

Kao's sitting up, and Uncle Marcus is seated at the foot of the bed. Noah's slouched in a chair, staring at his phone.

"Hey," I say as I walk inside, and I first go to hand Noah his burger.

"Thanks, you're a lifesaver."

Kao's head snaps in my direction, and a frown forms on his forehead. I have to gather all my strength to move to the side of the bed. The lines on his face deepen as I lean down. I press a kiss to his cheek, but a second later, he turns his face away from me.

As I straighten up, Jase places his arm around my waist and pulls me into his side.

I watch as Mila hugs Kao, and it hurts like hell when he hugs her back.

No matter how strong I try to be, it's too much. Lifting a hand to my face, I cover my mouth as I pull away from

Jase. I leave the room in a hurry, fighting to keep the tears back.

Darting down the hallway, I rush to the waiting room, praying it's empty. The moment I walk inside, a sob escapes me.

"I'm so sorry, Fallon," Mila says behind me, and then she comes to hug me.

I wrap my arms around my friend while I try my best to swallow the heartbreaking emotions back. I suck in a deep breath and then pull away from her.

"I'm fine." I force a smile to my face as I meet her eyes.

I'm not okay. Not even a little.

KAO

It kills me being cold toward Fallon. I so badly want to hold her but keeping her at a distance is best. She'll get over me in no time, and then she can move on with her life.

"Why are you doing this, Kao?" Jase snaps angrily.

I shake my head, not having the strength to face off with Fallon's cousin again. Earlier today was enough to drain me.

I feel Jase move closer to me, and then he grinds out, "Answer me."

I let out an exhausted sigh. "Drop it, Jase."

"Drop it? Seriously?" he growls. "You just fucking hurt Fallon in front of me! You're walking around blind when you can get your sight back. I won't fucking drop it."

"Do we have to do this now?" I snap.

"Yes. Explain to me why you're behaving like a total asshole? Why won't you go for the surgery? Why did you push Fallon away?"

I press my lips together, refusing to answer his questions. The second Jase finds out why I'm doing this, he won't back down. I'd rather let him think I'm a bastard.

I feel Jase's eyes burn on me. "This affects the whole group, and Mila's just been through hell. We all have. I won't have you upsetting Mila and Fallon more. They're worried out of their minds, and so are the rest of us."

I know Jase is right, and it tears me in half. I need to protect Fallon, but I don't want to cause my friends any further pain.

To my surprise, Dad says, "Kao said he'd think about it."

I can't bear seeing what I've done to Fallon. I just can't.

"Sorry, Mr. Reed, but thinking about it isn't enough." Then Jase snaps at me, "Just tell us what's going on. God, none of this makes any sense."

I clench my jaw, keeping my eyes and mouth shut.

If I thought that would be enough to deter Jase, I'm sorely mistaken.

"Kao, don't fucking sit there and ignore me. I'll stand here until you speak to me."

To make matters worse, Noah asks, "Are we finally having an intervention?"

"Fuck," I grumble. "Would you all just back off?"

"Nope." Again Noah lets the 'P' pop, and it has me fisting my hands to keep from responding.

"We're here because we love you, Kao," Dad tries to reassure me.

A couple of seconds of silence pass, then Jase shouts, "Kao! Stop this fucking shit!"

My eyes snap open, and even though I can't see anything, I glare in Jase's direction. My anger spirals out of control and darting to my feet, I yell, "I hurt Fallon! Okay?

96

Are you fucking happy now?" My breaths rush over my lips, and every muscle in my body is tense.

"Far from," Jase growls. "That doesn't explain shit to me."

"I hurt her," I grind the words out. "She's scarred because of me!" I shake my head as all the guilt whirls with my anger, and it creates a turbulent storm inside me. "I was supposed to keep her safe."

"Hold on," Jase says, and I hear him move closer until his voice sounds up right in front of me, "Are you refusing the transplant because you feel guilty?"

Fuck. I should've kept my mouth shut.

"Is Jase right?" Dad asks.

When I don't say anything, one of them places a hand on my shoulder. I realize it's Jase when he says, "Kao, that's the same as me taking the blame for what happened to Mila."

I shake my head hard. "I was the one driving."

"The truck driver caused the accident," Dad says. "You did everything you could to keep Fallon safe. You took the full brunt of the impact."

"You're going to punish yourself by staying blind? That's bullshit," Jase grumbles. "You're putting us all through hell because of misplaced guilt."

Jase is like a dog with a bone, and it has me admitting, "I can't face seeing what I've done to her."

A bark of laughter bursts from Jase. "So you're going to hide from it? Seriously?" His grip on my shoulder tightens, and I feel him lean closer. "I fucking manned up and stood by Mila. I was the one who took her nightmares, her fucking broken body, her agony, and fear. I'm the one who heard her cries, and they will haunt me forever," he bites out. "But not once did I hide from it. Grow a fucking pair and do the same for Fallon."

His words knock the breath from my lungs.

Fuck. Jase is right.

He didn't back down once. He stood by Mila like an indestructible force.

Fuck, I was taking the easy way out, not wanting to face what I did to Fallon. I'm such a fucking coward.

But I still won't saddle her with my being blind.

"I still can't be with Fallon," I admit.

"Why?" Jase demands.

"Even if I go through with the transplant, there's a chance it won't work."

"Ten percent," Noah argues. "The odds are good you'll see again. Let's focus on the positive."

"Still," I take a deep breath, trying to breathe through the hell raging inside me, "Too much can go wrong. I won't tie Fallon down with a disabled man."

"Let's deal with that when it happens," Jase says. "Just be a friend to her until you know for sure. No one's forcing you to date her."

Easier said than done. Will I be able to just be a friend to her?

Jase must see something on my face because he continues, "Are you done being an idiot now? Will you have the transplant?"

Knowing I don't stand a chance against Jase, Noah, and Dad, I nod.

"Thank fuck," Noah mumbles.

I feel Dad rise to his feet. "So I can tell Dr. Davis to go ahead and schedule the surgery?"

"Yeah," I mutter.

If the surgery is successful, I'll just have to face what I've done.

Chapter 8

FALLON

Anxiety claws it's way up my spine as Mom begins to peel back the dressing from my cheek.

My eyes keep darting between the mirror and the counter, not sure whether I can handle seeing the cuts. When I see the first glimpse of red, I shut my eyes tightly.

Mom pauses for a moment. "It's going to be okay. Dr. Menard will remove all the scarring. I've seen his work, and he's really the best."

I nod and swallow hard as Mom continues to remove the bandage. When she's done, she wraps her arm around my shoulder and says, "It's looking so much better already."

I take a deep breath, and fisting my hands at my sides, I push through the anxiety and open my eyes.

Oh, God.

The ground rips open beneath my feet as my gaze settles on the haphazard red cuts and stitches. I look like something from a horror movie. Random gashes mar my skin all the way from my cheek down to my neck.

Absolute revulsion shudders through me, and I gasp, "Mommy."

Mom's hold on me tightens, and she moves between the mirror and me. Her eyes lock on mine, and I see the heartache she feels for me shimmering in them. "Dr. Menard is the best. He'll make it all go away," she tries to reassure me.

"I look like a monster," I cry.

I can't deal with this.

"Let's get it cleaned and covered again. Okay?" Mom says, and she hurries through the routine.

My eyes are glued to the mirror. It feels like the woman in me has been cut out of me.

I'm disfigured.

All I can manage are shallow breaths. Mom carefully puts on fresh bandages, and once she's done, her arms wrap tightly around me. "I promise I'll make sure every last scar is gone. Okay?"

Stuck in a haze of disgust and shock, I nod.

Even though the cuts are covered, I can still see them clearly. They're hideous.

I'm ugly.

Bile pushes up my throat, and pulling free from Mom, I rush to the toilet. My body heaves as I vomit from the sight of my face.

Mom's hand settles on my back as I empty my stomach. Once I sit back, sobs begin to wrack through me.

I'll never be able to show my face in public.

Mourning the loss of my perfect life, I have no idea how I'll ever be able to accept living as a disfigured woman.

Woman?

No.

No longer.

I'm nothing more than a monster.

KAO

I get to go home for three days before I have to return for the surgery.

Dad argued that I should give school a break. I know it doesn't make sense that I return to Trinity because I can't attend classes. Still, I want to be in my own space. I know exactly where everything is in the suite.

Noah helps me up to the suite. I hear him shut the door behind us, and then Mila says, "Welcome back." Her arms wrap around me.

When she pulls back, someone else hugs me, then Jade mumbles, "I missed you."

"Thanks, girls." I tighten my hold on Noah's arm. "I'm just going to head to my room."

Noah leads me down the hallway, and when he shuts the door behind us, I let out a heavy breath.

I recall where everything is and head in the direction of the bed. When I bump into it, Noah says, "We should check how many steps there are between everything. If you memorize it, you should be able to move around better."

"Okay." I sit down on the side of the bed.

"One. Two…"

"Are you doing it now?" I ask.

"Might as well," Noah states, and then he continues to count. "Okay, so there are seven steps between the door and the bed."

"Got it."

I hear him move around, and then he says, "Five from the bedside table to the bathroom and then five to the toilet."

I let out a chuckle. "Got it."

"From the foot of the bed to your closet is four to the right, then five forward.

"I'm not going to remember it all."

"We'll run through it a couple of times. Get up," Noah orders.

Groaning, I rise to my feet, and we begin to practice walking around the room I've been living in the past four years.

I hear the door open. "Look who's home," Jase says. All the aggression from the fight is gone, and he sounds like his old self again. "Welcome back." Then he asks, "What are you doing?"

"I'm helping Kao get used to moving around the room," Noah explains.

"Need help?"

"Sure," Noah answers. "Go stand by the bathroom."

Noah leads me back to the bed. "You're on the right side of the bed. I'll be at the walk-in closet."

"And?" I ask, not sure what they expect me to do.

"It's five steps to Jase. Let's see if you can do it," Noah instructs.

I shrug and take five careful steps. Jase lets out a burst of laughter right by me. "You did it. Fucking awesome."

"Now it should be six steps to me," Noah says, sounding a little proud.

I turn to my right and count six steps, but halfway through the sixth one, I walk into Noah, and he instantly grips hold of my arms. "Okay, so it's five and a half."

"What are you all doing?" I hear Hunter ask.

"Hey, you're just in time. Stay right there," Jase answers him. "Kao's learning how many steps to take to get around the room."

Noah turns me in a quarter circle. "Four to the right, seven forward to get to Hunter."

I don't feel as unsure as I did when we started this practice and walk a little faster. When I should be standing by Hunter, I ask, "And? Did I do it right?"

"Yeah," Hunter murmurs, his voice hoarse. "You totally did it. I'm right here." I feel him take hold of my arm.

"Great, let's do this again," Noah orders.

"How many times?" I ask.

"Until you can do it without me having to remind you of how many steps to take."

I keep practicing the steps until it feels like I'm almost walking normally.

"Now for the rest of the suite," Noah says, popping my little bubble of pride.

"Are you serious?" I ask. "Can't we take a break?"

"Nope."

"You gotta stop popping your 'p' like that," I complain.

"Nope," the fucker teases me.

"Where do you want us?" Jase asks.

"Jase, you stand at the end of the hallway. Hunter, you take the kitchen."

Noah guides me into the hallway, then I hear Mila ask, "What are you doing?"

"We're helping Kao get used to moving around the suite," Jase fills her in.

"Can I help?"

"Sure," Noah answers. "You can go stand in the living room."

"Hold up," Mila says, and then she calls out, "Jade, Hana, Fallon, get your butts out here."

Fuck.

"What's up?" Jade asks.

"Yeah?" I hear Hana.

"Where's Fallon?" Mila asks.

"She's... sleeping," Hana answers. I don't miss the pause, and it makes me think Fallon might be avoiding me. Not that I can complain. It's what I wanted.

Still sucks, though.

"Hana, go stand by the front door and Jade, stand in front of Kao's room."

When everybody's taken their positions, Noah walks through the suite with me, counting all the different steps. It feels like hours have passed by the time I have an idea of how far apart everything is.

Before I can head back toward my room, Jase takes hold of my arm. "You need to talk to Fallon."

I know. It's unavoidable.

I suck in a deep breath, then nod.

"Fifteen steps to her door," Jase murmurs.

Reaching to my left so I can feel the wall, I take the fifteen steps. When I feel the door, I glance back to where Jase is.

"Yeah, just knock," he answers my silent question.

I take a moment to steel myself. It's going to gut me talking to Fallon, but it has to be done. I knock on the door,

107

and when there's no answer, I say, "Hana said she's sleeping. I'll try later again."

I begin to turn in the direction of my own room when I hear the door open, and her scent drifts to me. Sucking it up, I ask, "Can we talk?"

"Yeah," she answers softly, her voice sounding broken.

Hearing how she's hurting sends a wave of pain through my chest.

Knowing the layout of Fallon's bedroom and that it's always clean, I take five steps inside, then pause.

I hear her shut the door and feel her move closer to me.

"I'm glad you agreed to have the surgery," she says, sounding anxious.

Christ, I hate that she's uncomfortable around me.

When I remain silent, Fallon asks, "What do you want to talk about?"

She sounds exhausted and... raw.

"It can wait until you feel better," I answer.

She lets out a sigh. "The bed is to your left. Can I help you?"

I reach a hand in her direction, and when her fingers wrap around mine, and I move closer to her, my self-restraint slips, and I almost give in to my need to hold her.

She helps me to the bed, and it serves as a wake-up call. This is precisely what I don't want for Fallon – her having to look after my grown-ass as if I'm a baby.

I sit down and then try to gather my thoughts.

"It's been a shit week," I mutter, not sure how to start this conversation.

"Yeah," she agrees.

I feel her sit down next to me.

"Do you know when the surgery will be?" Fallon asks.

"Thursday." Leaning forward, I rest my forearms on my thighs and clasp my hands together. "I'm sorry."

I'm so fucking sorry.

"You have a lot to deal with," she excuses my behavior.

Shaking my head, I suck in a deep breath, and then I ask the question I've been dreading, "Can we go back to being friends?"

I hear her swallow. "What do you mean?"

Fuck, this is hard.

"Just friends, Fallon. Nothing more." The words weigh a ton. It's filled with remorse, heartache, and loss. I know she'll keep fighting for us if I don't force her to walk away from me, and it has me lying, "It's not like we dated. We weren't in a relationship. We're just going back to the way things were."

"But…" I hear her breaths speed up. "You asked me on a date. There was more between us," she argues.

My stubborn fighter.

I close my eyes as another wave of pain moves through me.

I don't want to let you go.

But I don't have a choice.

"Yeah, that was a mistake," I keep lying. "We were never meant to be more than friends."

"How can you say that?" she gasps. "I know you love me, Kao. I saw it in your eyes. I felt it in your hugs."

God help me. I'm not strong enough to break her heart.

Getting up from the bed, I thrust a hand through my hair.

Fuck, this is killing me.

"Of course I love you, Fallon," I admit one truth before I continue with the lies, "As a friend. Nothing more."

I hear her breath hitch, and my arms yearn to comfort her.

"How can you stand there and say there was nothing more than friendship between us?" she snaps.

It's good that she's getting angry. It will help her deal with the heartache.

Before I can answer her, Fallon continues, "What about all the things you said last Wednesday? You asked me on a date, Kao. Yeah, you wanted to take things slow, but… you asked me on the date."

"I made a mistake." I let out a sigh. All the lying is gutting me wide open. It feels like my soul is hemorrhaging. "I… We've always gotten along. I think with Hunter and Jade, and then Jase and Mila pairing up, I got caught up in the moment."

Fuck, this is so unfair. Why did that truck have to hit us? Why did this happen to us?

I shake my head, the questions only filling my chest with more despair.

My heart cracks right down the middle as I say, "I care for you the same way I care for the other girls. I'm sorry I let you think otherwise."

I hear her get up, and then she comes to stand in front of me. I can feel her gaze on me and lower my eyes in the direction of the floor.

Her hand touches my jaw, and then she nudges my face up. "Don't look down and tell me we're nothing more than friends."

I pull back from her touch and gathering the last of my strength, I keep my voice low and cold as I say, "Stop

111

digging for something that's not there, Fallon! I don't have to justify my feelings to you. Fucking drop it already. I'm trying to save our friendship."

"I..." I hear her suck in a trembling breath. "I just don't understand."

"What's there to understand?" I snap, needing to end this conversation. "I never should've asked you on the date. We shouldn't have been on that road, to begin with."

Needing to leave because I can't stomach hurting her more than I already have, I walk in the direction I think the door is. My hand smacks against the wood, and I feel for the knob. As I let myself out, I hear Fallon's breath hitch before a soft sob escapes her.

Closing my eyes, it's almost impossible to leave her, but I somehow manage. Shutting the door behind me, I stumble in a broken stupor towards my own bedroom.

My heart feels shredded, but I keep telling myself it's for the best. I can't offer Fallon the future she deserves.

It's for the best.

She'll find someone who will be able to give her the world.

Once I close the door behind me, I sink to the floor, and I shove both my hands through my hair. I try to breathe past the unbearable pain until I lower a hand to claw at my chest.

It fucking hurts. So much.

God, why didn't I die?

Chapter 9

FALLON

I have to meet with Dr. Menard at eleven am. You'd think it would be the only thing on my mind, but it's not. I'm still trying to process everything that's happened. My emotions are all over the place.

Kao's words. They keep shredding my heart to pieces.

My guilt is eating away at me, destroying the last of my spirit. I shouldn't have told Kao to take that route to the restaurant. The accident could've been avoided if I'd kept my mouth shut.

Kao blames me.

Through the turbulent mess inside me, fear taints everything with despairing shadows. How am I going to adjust to life with scars? A life without Kao?

While I try to make sense of everything, I'm constantly bombarded with memories of us, which hurt me even more.

My stomach is knotted with nerves as I walk toward Kao, where he's sitting with the other guys in the living room. We're all at Jase's place for a barbeque. My prom's this coming Friday, and I'm out of time. Either I ask Kao to escort me, or I'll have to go alone.

Guys from school have asked me, but I said no to them all. There's only one man I have eyes for, and I'm inches from him.

Kao's striking gaze drifts to me, and the corner of his mouth lifts. He's so attractive it stuns me for a moment.

"Where are the other girls?" Jase asks, yanking my attention away from Kao.

The smile on my face trembles from the nervousness pulsing through me as I answer, "The girls are still out back talking about what they're wearing to the prom." Turning my gaze to Kao, I ask, "Can we talk?"

A slight frown forms on his forehead as he places his drink on the table. "Sure."

I gesture to the front door. "Is outside okay?"

The other guys stare at us, and it makes me even more anxious. When Kao stands up, I spin around and hurry out of Jase's place. I take the steps down the porch and head in the direction of the rock garden.

Lights make the backyard look like a fairyland, but I'm too busy trying to control my breathing to take in any of it.

Reaching the water feature that's nestled between boulders, I swallow hard before I turn to face Kao, where he stopped behind me. His eyes shine like polished sapphires in the moonlight.

"So... uhm," I struggle to think of the right words. I've practiced what I'd say a hundred times, and now I can't remember anything.

Kao reaches for me, and his strong fingers wrap around my arm. "Are you okay?"

I nod and suck in a trembling breath. "Yeah, I just... I want to ask you something."

Concern still darkens Kao's features, and then an encouraging smile tugs at his mouth. "What can I help with?"

My eyes drift over Kao's features, and once again, I'm left breathless by how handsome he is. Add how kind and caring he is, and it's hard to believe he's not an angel.

"Ah..." I stammer, "my prom is this coming Friday," I begin. Wanting to do this right, I square my shoulders and lift my chin a little higher. "Will you go with me?"

For a moment, Kao looks puzzled, then a smile spreads over his face. "Damn, I was worried there for a second. Is that all you wanted to ask?"

I nod, fear that he'll say no, making my eyes lock on his mouth.

"I'd be honored to, Fallon," his lips form the magical words I've been dying to hear.

I let out a breath of relief as my mouth splits into a wide smile.

Kao still looks puzzled as he asks, "Have none of the guys from school asked you?"

"There were a couple," I admit. "But I didn't want to go with any of them. I want my prom to be perfect."

Kao lets out a chuckle. "And I'm the only guy who will let you dress him up, right?"

I roll my eyes. "That's not the only reason."

"Well, let me know what I should wear and what time I have to pick you up."

I grin at Kao, and unable to resist, I throw my arms around his neck and give him a hug. "Thank you. It means a lot to me that you said yes."

Kao's arms wrap around me, and it makes a kaleidoscope of butterflies flutter to life in my stomach.

With Kao by my side, my prom will be a dream come true.

A tear sneaks out of my eye and soon disappears into the bandage.

Since the prom, Kao's been... my person.

I'm drowning in misery when there's a knock at my door, and Hana walks into my room.

She takes one look at me then comes to give me a hug. "Hey, my friend." Her voice is filled with compassion and love.

"Hey," I murmur.

Hana pulls back and sits down next to me on the bed. "How are you holding up?"

I shake my head. I'd typically act strong around everyone. But with my family, Hana, Jase, and Hunter, I don't have to. They're the closest to me, and I don't have to pretend with them.

"It... it hurts so much," I admit, and a sob escapes my lips. I press the back of my hand to my mouth. Hana spent the whole night with me after the devastating conversation with Kao.

She wraps me up in a hug. "I don't get it as well. Anyone could see Kao loved you. I wish I knew why he's so distant with you."

When I pull back, I unload all my heartache on my best friend. "I think he blames me for the accident." A sob shudders through me. "I told him to take that route."

Shaking my head, I mutter, "If only I'd kept my mouth shut."

Hana shakes her head. "It's not your fault, Fallon. Don't blame yourself." She lets out a sigh. "Maybe Kao doesn't want to saddle you with his disability. Then again, the transplant will give him his vision back. None of it makes any sense."

"Or it could be the scars," I gasp. "They're hideous. No guy would want to be with someone who looks like me." My chin trembles and more tears flow over my cheeks.

"Don't, Fallon. You're not hideous." Hana pulls me back into a hug. "Your dad's taking you to the doctor's appointment, right?"

"Yeah." Pulling back, I meet Hana's gaze. "What if it doesn't work? What if it makes the scars worse?"

"Dr. Menard's the best. I'm sure the surgery will be a success," Hana tries to encourage me.

"I'll still have some scarring."

"You'll still be my beautiful friend," Hana says.

"Kao might not think so," I whisper. Since Kao's strong reaction to my injuries and the conversation we had yesterday, my self-esteem is practically non-existent.

"I'm sure Kao doesn't think that." Hana gets up and says, "Take deep breaths. Your dad will be here any second."

I do my best to calm down, and when I've managed to regain some control over my disastrous emotions, I rise to my feet. I lift my chin, and taking a last deep breath, I leave the room with Hana at my side.

Walking into the living room, I instantly notice Kao where he's sitting on the couch next to Noah.

The sight of him threatens to knock my feet from under me, but somehow I manage to keep my composure. I force a smile to my lips. "Hey, guys."

Noah's head snaps up from his laptop. "Hey. Are you going to the doctor's appointment?"

"Yeah."

Just then, there's a knock at the front door. Hana goes to open for my father.

Dad steps inside, and just seeing him makes the tears threaten to fall. While Noah and Kao greet him, I hurry out of the suite, not able to keep my composure for much longer.

———————————

KAO

Noah's trying to keep me up to date with classes by talking through the material with me.

"Should we do the assignment?" he asks. "Then I can submit it on your behalf."

I turn my head in Noah's direction as a wave of thankfulness washes over me. I haven't felt many good emotions the past week, and it makes me over-emotional.

Lifting my hand, I move it over to Noah, and once I feel his forearm, I grip him tightly. Clearing my throat, I murmur, "Thank you." I turn to Noah and pull him into a hug. "Thank you for everything. I know I've been a dick, but God, I would not survive this without you."

He wraps one arm around me. "I'll always have your back."

"I know." I swallow hard. "And it means everything to me."

We've just pulled apart when I hear Jade ask, "Guys, you want coffee?"

The corner of my mouth lifts. "That would be awesome." Jade and Mila take turns checking if I want something to drink or eat. It's fucking humbling how hard my friends are trying to make things easier for me.

I hear more movement, and then Jase asks, "Are we having lunch at the restaurant today? I think you should start getting out."

And then there's Jase, always pushing me. He means well, and I know I can't hide forever. I need to find a new routine, a new way of living.

Silence follows his question, and it feels like everyone is holding their breaths as they wait for my response.

Then Jase says, "I'll even fucking clear out the restaurant. I just don't want you holing up in the suite."

I let out a chuckle because Jase would turn this campus upside down for any of his friends.

"You don't have to. But can we go either before or after the lunch rush?"

"Hell yeah!" Jase lets out, probably happy that I didn't fight him on it.

"We can go at eleven?" Jade mentions. "Or at two? It should be quieter then." She lets out a huff. "And I'll freaking punch anyone who looks sideways at you."

I let out a bark of laughter. There's no doubt in my mind Jade would do that. She's fierce as fuck when it comes to us.

"Let's make it for two," Jase says. "That way, Fallon will be back from her doctor's appointment."

Instantly my worry for her shoots through me like a rocket, extinguishing the calmness I just felt.

"Here's your coffee," Jade murmurs, and then I feel her take hold of my hand. She guides my fingers closer and waits for me to take hold of the cup.

"Got it," I say. "Thanks."

"How did the conversation go with Fallon?" Jase suddenly asks.

"Not as well as I hoped it would," I admit, knowing Jase probably knows already that I practically ripped Fallon's heart out.

Just thinking about yesterday tears my heart wide open again.

Not wanting to get into the details with Jase, I say, "We'll get back to being friends again. Don't worry about it."

Noah's been typing non-stop during the conversation, and it has me asking, "Are you doing my assignment?"

"Just the basics, then we can work on it together," he mumbles.

Jase lets out a chuckle. "Noah, you're unbelievable. Kao can thank his lucky stars for you."

Smiling, I add, "For all of you. You've all helped a hell of a lot. I really appreciate it."

"That's what friends are for," Jase says. I hear him move. "I better get my ass to class." Then he hollers, "Hunter, let's go!"

I listen to my friends moving around the suite, which lulls me into a sense of calm.

Honestly, I'd be fucked without them. They make the darkness bearable.

"Okay, let's do this," Noah says, drawing my attention to him.

We work on the assignment until it's done, but my thoughts stay with Fallon. I wonder if the appointment is going well and if she's okay.

When the front door opens, I turn my head slightly in its direction.

"You're back," Noah says. "How did it go?"

"Good," Fallon answers.

"What did the doctor say?" Noah asks the question that's burning on the tip of my tongue.

"He was optimistic. He can only schedule the surgery in January." I can hear the ache straining Fallon's words. "All and all the feedback was good."

Fallon's not telling us everything, and I almost ask her what it is, but I know I have no right.

"We're all going for lunch at two," Noah informs her.

"I'm going to pass. I'm tired after the appointment. Have fun, though."

I hear her walk away from us, and then her bedroom door shuts.

"How does she look?" I ask Noah.

"I haven't seen the cuts. She's still wearing a bandage," he tells me.

"I mean emotionally? Is she okay?"

Noah pauses for a moment, then he murmurs, "She looks terrible, Kao. She's not coping."

My body jerks with the instinct to get up and go after her. I want to comfort her so badly, it's tightening every muscle.

But I remain seated, knowing I'm the last person she needs right now.

"Don't worry. Hana's with her," Noah says as if he can sense my internal struggle.

Noah starts to go through more of the work I missed, but I'm hardly paying attention.

Staying away from Fallon is fucking hard. I have no idea how long I'm going to manage to keep up with the act.

125

As much as I need my friends, I might have to consider leaving the academy.

Fuck, who would've thought this is how the year would turn out? I think back to the day the girls moved in.

I remember the welcome ball and how beautiful Fallon looked? Images of her flash through my mind, and I find relief in them. They lessen the dark.

I was going to ask Summer to accompany me to the welcome ball, but after Jase said we should all go as a group, I let that idea sail. Also, the girls didn't seem to get along with Summer and her friends. That's how I automatically became Fallon's plus one.

As I walk out of my room, my eyes lock onto Fallon, where she's a couple of steps ahead of me, heading toward the living room. My breath catches in my throat. She looks fucking beautiful in a silver dress that matches my charcoal suit. My gaze drifts down her perfect body, stopping at her ass.

Damn, she's sexy as fuck.

There's a sharp burst of attraction, and I'm unable to tear my eyes away from her.

"Mila, can you help me with my necklace?" Fallon asks as she steps into the open space, yanking me out of my thoughts.

126

"I'll help," the words rush from me as I come up behind her. Moving to stand in front of Fallon, I take the necklace from her hand. I open the clasp, and taking a step closer to her, I first brush her hair to the side. Her soft scent spins a web around me, and unable to stop myself, I lean in close until our cheeks brush, and I clasp the necklace in place.

Awareness grows in my chest, and a current zaps between us. Pausing for a moment, I take a deep breath of Fallon as the attraction increases. It's over-powering.

I've always thought Fallon was beautiful, and yeah, we're good friends, but since she moved into the suite and we've seen each other every day, I've realized I feel more than friendship for her.

A hell of a lot more.

Pulling back, I let my gaze drift over her before I meet her eyes. "You look breathtaking, Fallon."

Her lips curve into a smile. "Thanks, Kao." A nervous expression pulls around her mouth, and she fiddles with the necklace. "You almost look like an adult in the suit." Then she darts to where Hunter is sitting, and it makes the corner of my mouth lift. Fallon doesn't get nervous often, and knowing it's because of me gives me hope that she feels the attraction as well.

The corners of my mouth curve up at the memory. That night Jade and Mila grilled me to ask Fallon on a date, but I was more than happy just holding her in my arms and dancing with her.

At least I have my memories. My eyes drift shut, thinking they'll have to last me a lifetime.

Chapter 10

FALLON

Dr. Menard is optimistic that he can remove all the scarring. It gives me some hope, but until the surgery in late January, I'll have to live with them.

The appointment made me feel better, but right now, the loss of Kao is overshadowing everything.

Yesterday the heartache was sharp, but as the initial sting lessened, the ache became unrelenting.

It's uncanny how you don't realize how much you love someone until they're gone.

But Kao's not gone. He's here, and it serves as a constant reminder of what I've lost. Seeing his flawless face, his striking blue eyes still brings a rush of attraction every time I look at him.

When he laughs with the others, and he talks with them as if nothing has changed, it rips out another piece of my soul.

I know he loved me. Nothing he says will change that belief. But he also blames me for the accident, and I know I'm guilty. Me and my control-freak ways destroyed our relationship before it even had a chance to start.

I don't think I'll ever heal from the hole it ripped through my life.

Kao was, is, and will be the only man for me.

Thinking about the empty future stretching ahead of me makes hopelessness grow in my chest.

I'll never feel his kiss.

I'll never make love to him.

God, will I even get to hug him again?

"Fallon," Hana whispers as she sits down next to me.

I shut my eyes against the unrelenting ache that's slowly driving me insane.

"I can't, Hana," I murmur, my voice tight from all the heartache. "I can't imagine my life without him."

Hana wraps her arms around me. "I'm sure things will come right between the two of you as soon as he has his sight back," she tries to reassure me.

Shaking my head, I suck in a trembling breath. "I don't think so. Kao doesn't do or say anything without thinking it through. If he felt we could get through this, he wouldn't have pulled away from me." Realizing he's really done with me makes a pain-filled gasp rush over my lips.

My body cramps from the heartache, and all I can do is cry. There's no relief from the tears.

Only the incessant anguish.

I'll have to learn to live with it, or at the very least, to pretend I'm fine.

Pulling back from Hana, I get up and walk to the bathroom. I wet a facecloth under the cold water, then press it lightly over the left side of my face, removing all traces that I've been crying.

Lifting my gaze to the mirror, I stare at my eyes.

Pull yourself together, Fallon. Life goes on, with or without you.

I now understand why Mila pretended to be okay.

You can do it, too. Chin up. Brave face.

No one has to know you're dying inside.

———————————

"Family fun time," Jade yells from the living room.

"Come on. We can do with a bit of fun," Hana says.

I follow her out of the door, and when we walk into the living room, I notice the bottle of whiskey, tumblers, and Jase's phone on the coffee table.

"Truth or drink?" I ask, while my eyes dart over the open spaces to sit. Usually, I'd go sit next to Kao, and even though there's space for me, I don't think it would be a good idea.

I follow Hana and take a seat next to her.

"Tonight's game is a little different. *Would you rather.* The arrow will spin and whoever it lands on has a turn to answer. It's just to ease the tension," Jase explains.

I watch Mila snuggle into his side, then my eyes move to Hunter and Jade. There's an intense pang of loss seeing them happy together.

I wanted that with Kao.

"It's probably going to be inappropriate," Noah chuckles.

Jase grins. "Of course." Then he pours a shot of whiskey for everyone.

I'm not a big drinker, but right now, the amber liquid is a welcome relief.

When everyone is ready, Jase presses spin, and the arrow lands on Hunter.

Mila checks her phone, then she lets out a chuckle, "Would you rather live without your girlfriend or your best friend?"

"Fuck," Hunter grumbles. "I'm in shit no matter what I answer. Can I just drink?"

"Yeah, but you have to down two shots. One for me and one for Jade."

"How do you figure that?" Hunter asks, right before he downs the first tumbler.

"Oh, it's just because I want to get your ass drunk," Jase laughs. He presses spin on the screen again, and it lands on Noah.

The grin on Mila's face grows as she asks, "Would you rather date someone five years older or five years younger?"

"Older." Noah didn't even have to think about the answer. Reaching over, he presses start, and I begin to grimace as the arrow slows until it stops on me.

Damn.

"Would you rather marry someone you know nothing about or someone from your group of friends?" Mila asks.

This isn't fun at all.

I force a smile to my face, and looking at Hana, I try to joke, "You want to marry me?"

"Sure," she grins, wagging her eyebrows at me.

Needing strength to get through this game, I pour myself some whiskey and let the liquid burn down my throat while the arrow stops on Mila.

"Crap," she mutters under her breath, probably already knowing what the next question is, seeing as she has the list. She scrunches her nose, then reads, "Would you rather have a baby now or never?"

Before she can answer, Jase says, "Guess we're leaving y'all to go make a baby."

His reaction draws laughter from us all, and it helps to ease the tension hanging in the air like a suffocating cloud.

When the arrow lands on Kao, my eyes dart between him and Mila.

"Would you rather have sex with a friend or a stranger?"

His eyebrow raises at the question, and not taking a moment to think, which he usually would do, he answers, "A friend."

"There's a lot I'd do for you, but that's a solid hell no," Noah mutters.

Everyone laughs until Jase asks, "Which one of us?"

Kao tilts his head in Jase's direction, and his features tighten. "I can't see shit, so it doesn't really matter." Kao gets up, and feeling his way around the couch, I watch as he leaves.

"Well, that didn't work," Mila murmurs, a sad frown between her brows.

My eyes dart over my friends, and seeing the strain on their faces makes a new worry grow in me.

Are we going to survive, or will this accident rip us all apart?

KAO

I've only been back at the hospital for an hour, and already I'm nauseous from the disinfectant clinging to every surface.

Last night was one of the longest of my life. I kept wavering between feeling hopeful and scared out of my mind.

Dr. Davis checks my eyes, then begins to explain, "You won't be able to see right after the surgery."

"And after?" Dad asks from where he's sitting next to the bed.

"Kao," Dr. Davis addresses me, "you'll have to wear dark prescription sunglasses, and you'll have to sleep with the eye shields on to protect the cornea against rubbing. Your eyes will be light-sensitive, and you'll probably get headaches. At first, you'll see shades of black and gray. You'll be able to see a person, but not what they look like. Gradually color and the finer details will return. After two months, you should be able to see well, and your sight will start to settle."

"How long will the whole process take?" I ask. Dr. Davis sounds confident that I'll see again, and it stirs hope in my chest.

Maybe.

"Six to twelve weeks," Dr. Davis answers. He gives my shoulder a squeeze. "I'll see you in the operating room."

I nod, and after he's left, Dad's voice is optimistic as he says, "It all sounds good. How do you feel?"

Too scared to let the hope in. I won't survive the crushing blow of being blind a second time.

"I'm good," I lie, even trying to curve my lips into a smile.

After a while, a nurse comes to get me. When I'm lying on a bed in the operating room, and I hear the medical staff move around me, my heartbeat begins to speeds up.

136

I start to breathe faster and grip the covers tightly.

Fuck. The hope took root. What if it doesn't work?

Panic builds in my chest as the fear fills my mind.

I feel fingers wrap around my hand. "I'm here, my angel-boy."

Hearing my godmother's voice makes a lump rush up my throat. Even though she's a nurse at this hospital, I didn't expect her to be present at the surgery.

"Mamma G?" I ask, still not able to believe she's here.

"You're going to be just fine," she assures me. "If your daddy could do it, so can you."

I nod, feeling so much better now that I know she'll be here throughout the surgery. It sucks that I have to be awake for the procedure, but with my godmother here, it won't be as daunting.

"Thanks, Mamma G," I whisper, gripping her hand tighter. She's always been the heart of our circle of family and friends, but right now, she's everything. "Thank you."

I feel her press a kiss to my hand. "I love you my, angel-boy."

The procedure begins, and I try to focus on Miss Sebastian's fingers gripping mine. Every now and then, she gives me a squeeze.

I'm unable to take in any of the medical jargon as Dr. Davis works on my eyes.

Even though he said I won't see anything right away, I keep hoping to see a flash of light, a shadow... God, anything but this total black pit of hell.

———————

Dr. Davis said the surgery went well. I manage to get some sleep during the night, and when I wake up, it takes me a moment to remember the day before.

"Morning," I hear Miss Sebastian say happily. "It's about time you woke up. You almost missed breakfast." I hear cutlery, and then she asks, "Do you want some coffee, and then we can fight about how much you'll eat?"

Even though my eyes are painful, I let out a chuckle. "Coffee will be great."

Miss Sebastian waits for me to sit up, and then she adjusts the bed. Leaning back, I wait for her to hand me the coffee, and after taking a sip, I say, "Thanks for staying, Mamma G."

"My bedazzled ass wouldn't let my god-baby go through the surgery all by his lonesome."

"Mamma G," Noah grumbles from the couch where he slept, "did you know you snore?"

"I don't snore!" Miss Sebastian gasps. "I purr."

Noah lets out a chuckle. "Is there any coffee left?"

"Come get some."

"Aww… but you made Kao a cup," Noah complains. "I always knew he was your favorite."

"Don't make me get up and wack you into a different blood group," Miss Sebastian warns. "I love all my god-babies equally."

I hear her prepare a cup, and then Noah says, "Now I feel loved again."

"Little bedazzled shit," Miss Sebastian mumbles, then she turns her attention to me, and her voice is all sweet again as she says, "Time to eat."

Not having much of an appetite, I ask, "What's for breakfast?"

"Just toast. But lunch will be a whole different scenario," she warns.

"Are you staying the whole day?"

"I'm working the night shift for a co-worker that's on maternity leave. I took off yesterday for you, so my bedazzled ass needs to be back at work tonight."

Warmth spreads through my chest. "God, could I love you anymore?"

I hear the door, and then Dad says, "Morning. Wow, Miss Sebastian, it looks like something exploded in your hair."

"Don't start with me so early, Marcus. The ICU is only a couple of floors down."

I begin to laugh, loving it when she and Dad get into it with each other.

They keep bantering with each other until Dr. Davis walks into the room. The air instantly shifts from playful to tense.

I hear movement around the room, as Dr. Davis asks, "How do you feel today, Kao?"

Nervous as fuck.

"Besides the pain, I feel okay."

"Like I said yesterday, the surgery went well. You'll feel pain and irritation for some time. I'm going to remove the bandages today. During the first couple of days, the lights have to be dimmed, and the curtains closed to protect the cornea."

"How long will I have to do that?" I ask.

"A week at most. Wear sunglasses when you're outside. You might be sensitive to light. It differs from person to person."

Dr. Davis's fingers brush around my head as he begins to remove the bandage, and it sends my heart rate shooting through the ceiling. I feel Miss Sebastian's fingers grip mine, and I hold onto her for dear life.

"Remember, you might not see much, only shades of black and gray."

"Okay," I breathe the word out through my anxiety. Anything would be better than just the constant black.

Suddenly, apprehension fills my chest until it feels like the life is being squeezed out of me, and I almost call out for him to wait.

But then Miss Sebastian grips my hand tighter in both of hers, and I feel Dad's hand on my shin.

God. Please.

When the bandages are off, I keep my eyes closed.

I feel Dr. Davis' fingers on my right eyelid, and then he carefully pulls it up. A flash of gray slams the breath from my lungs. It was only for a moment. The flash is dimmer on my left side.

"Open your eyes," Dr. Davis instructs.

I begin to tremble from my emotions being all over the place, and when I slowly lift my lashes, there's nothing.

I begin to blink, and then I see dark shadows.

"Kao?" I hear the worry in Dad's voice.

"It's like I'm looking through a murky cloud of dark shadows," I try to explain as best I can.

"Every day it will get better," Dr. Davis assures me.

I glance in his direction, and when I manage to see the dark outline of a person, a breath shudders out of me. "Is that you, Dr. Davis?"

"Yes."

While Dr. Davis covers my eyes with the prescribed sunglasses, I alternate between feeling hopeful and worry that my vision won't recover enough for me to regain my independence.

One thing at a time, Kao. Take today as a win.

Chapter 11

FALLON

I stare at the update from Noah that just came through. They're on their way home. Noah's been sending me messages since Kao went back to the hospital. He's amazing for letting me know what's happening, but it's hard. I wish I could be with Kao.

Earlier, Noah said Kao could see shadows. It was such good news, but it was overshadowed by the fact that I can't celebrate with Kao.

I know he said we should be friends, but how am I suppose to be casual around him? I can't pretend I don't love him.

"Fallon," Hunter calls, ripping me out of my thoughts. "You have visitors."

I take a deep breath and force a smile to my face before I leave my room. When I walk into the living room and see my brother, Forest, it becomes harder to smile.

"Hey." There's a caring look on Forest's face as he comes to hug me. He might be a year younger than me, but he's so tall, I barely reach his shoulder. In a way, he's always been my big brother.

I wrap my arms around him and give myself a moment to enjoy the safety I feel in his embrace. When I pull back, I smile at Aria and Carla, Hunter and Jase's sisters. "What are you all doing here?"

"We wanted to see how you're doing," Forest explains.

Forest, Aria, and Carla are close like I am with Jase, Hunter, and Hana. But next year, the three of them will start at Trinity, and then we'll all probably become one big group.

Jase throws an arm around his little sister and asks, "How's school."

Carla glances up at him and shrugs, "Still sucks. I can't wait to start here."

Her answer draws a chuckle from Jase. "Yeah? Wait until you get your first assignments, and you'll be singing a different tune."

"I'm the clever one," she sasses her brother.

"Keep lying to yourself," he taunts her.

When we all keep standing, Hunter says, "Sit, guys."

I plop down on the nearest couch and watch as Forest waits for Aria to sit before he takes the seat next to her.

That used to be Kao and me.

Forest locks eyes with me for a second, and then his gaze moves to my cheek. "How do you feel?"

"I'm okay," I lie. "The stitches are coming out next week."

"Dad said Dr. Menard will be able to fix the cuts," he mentions.

"Yeah, the doctor is optimistic."

It's so hard to act normal, to communicate, to smile. I wish I could crawl into my bed and just stay there.

Forest begins to frown, and then he gets up. He gestures with his head toward the hallway, and when he walks in the direction of my room, I get up and follow him.

The instant I shut the door behind us, Forest asks, "How are you really doing?"

No matter how hard I try, I can't lie to my brother, and my face crumbles as the tears rush to the surface. I shake my head, and when Forest pulls me into a hug, sobs begin to wrack me.

Forest rubs a hand up and down my back. "Talk to me."

"I can't... deal with... everything," I admit. "It's too hard."

"What's everything?" he asks, his tone soft and caring, and it only makes the tears fall faster.

"Kao hates me. I look like a monster," I begin to ramble. "I can't keep up with the act. It's all too much."

Forest leads me over to the bed, and we sit down. He leans forward and tilting his head, he locks eyes with me. "You're not a monster, Fallon."

"You haven't seen the scars." A breath shudders out of my chest. Every morning I see my face is a death blow to my womanhood. "I can't even look at myself."

"Dad and Mom said the cuts are healing nicely."

I shake my head. "They're our parents. No matter how ugly we are, they'll love us."

A frown forms between Forest's eyebrows. "You're not ugly. Stop saying that."

"But it's the truth," I whimper.

I start to cry uncontrollably, and Forest quickly pulls me back into a hug. He tries to calm me with soothing words but none of them help. After a while, he asks, "Why don't you come home? It's just ten days until Christmas break. Mila or Jade can email you the work you'll miss out on."

I get up to go blow my nose. God, I've never cried this much before. My face feels swollen and tender.

Maybe Forest is right, and I should go home. I was wrong to think I'd be able to just go on with my life and ignore the brutal fact that it shattered to pieces. *Just like my face.*

When I sit down next to Forest again, I say, "The Christmas Ball is next week. At least everything's arranged, but I'll have to withdraw from the committee."

Forest places his arm around my shoulder. "I'll go to the office and take care of it. Start packing so I can take you home."

My chin begins to tremble again. I'm disappointed in myself. I thought I was stronger than this. But I know if I stay here I won't make it. I need to go home and be with my family. Right now, all our friends are worried about Kao, and they're focused on helping him. Rightly so. He's blind. My injuries are nothing compared to his... but still, I can't get through this on my own.

"Come on." Forest pulls me to my feet. "Just grab the stuff you'll need for the next two days. I'll take care of the rest."

I look up at my brother, and feeling broken and small, I wrap my arms around his waist and rest my left cheek against his chest. "Thank you."

He gives me a tight hug, then pulls back and smiles down at me. "Anything for my favorite sister."

I let out a chuckle. "I'm your only sister."

I move toward my walk-in closet. "I want to be gone before Kao gets back from the hospital."

"Okay. I'll run to the office. I'll be back in ten minutes."

Forest rushes out of the room, and I have to admit, I feel better knowing I'm going home.

KAO

I follow Noah into the suite but stop when he comes to a halt.

"I'm taking her home," I hear Forest's voice.

There's a moment's stunned silence, then Jase asks, "There's still a week and a half until Christmas break. What about her work?"

"And the Christmas Ball?" Mila adds.

"The lecturers will forward all her assignments, and the ball is the least of our worries," Forest states.

I hear movement, and then Jase asks, "Are you really going home?"

"Yeah," Fallon answers, her voice sounding fragile and soft.

I turn my head in her direction, wondering what the hell happened while I was gone. Besides the awkwardness between Fallon and me, things didn't seem so bad that she would leave. I was hoping for time, so I could at least salvage our friendship.

"I'll see you all after the Christmas break."

Noah pulls me to the side, then I hear him murmur, "Call if you need anything."

"Thanks, Noah," Fallon whispers near me.

A couple of seconds later, Noah says, "Let's get you to bed." He takes hold of my arm and begins to pull me toward the hallway.

I rear back and ask, "What happened?"

"Fallon just went home," Jase mutters.

"Because of me?" I hate asking the question, but if she's hurting so badly, then I have to do something. After all, we need to get back to being friends.

"Don't flatter yourself," Hana snaps as she passes by me. I hear the door slam shut behind her.

"Hana's just upset because of everything that's happened," Mila tries to cover for her friend. "We don't know why Fallon left. I'll check in with her once she's settled in at home."

I nod, hating that I'm no longer in a position to go after Fallon.

The campus and suite feel like a ghost town without Fallon.

I can't message her, and calling her while things are so volatile between us feels wrong. Over the past week, I've been seeing more blunt objects. I can make out a person and even the length of their hair.

"The swelling looks better," Noah murmurs as he puts in my eye drops. "The redness, as well."

"That's good." I grin at him. "I'm surprised how quickly the pain faded from post-surgery to today."

"How's the itchiness?" he asks.

"It comes and goes." Hopefully, that will be gone soon. When Noah is done, I put on my prescribed sunglasses. My eyes are still super sensitive to light, so for now, I stay indoors with the lights off.

"Let's get two hours work in before I have to go to class," Noah says. I can make out his frame as he moves around the room. Then he comes to sit next to me on the bed. "You have to make a business plan."

Adjusting after the surgery and catching up with the work I missed has become my new routine.

But life feels empty, and I know it's because Fallon's not here. Every second used to revolve around her. Seeing her smiles. Holding her hand. Just being with her even though we weren't dating.

And now there's nothing but work, eye drops, and praying my sight fully returns so I can get Fallon back.

I hate that she's missing the Christmas Ball. She worked so hard on all the preparations. I find myself spacing out, my memories of Fallon carrying me back to happier times when we attended the welcome function a couple of months ago.

Fallon crosses the floor toward our table. Reaching us, she locks eyes with me, her chin held high.

My God, she looks like a goddess.

"Kao, will you please open the dance floor with me?"

Surprise ripples through me. I know it's a huge deal who Fallon chooses to dance with, seeing as she's from one of the founding families at Trinity Academy.

151

I rise to my feet, and placing my hand on Fallon's lower back, I walk with her to the open space near the stage where the band is situated. As violin strings begin to fill the air, I capture her gaze, and I take her right hand in mine.

The song, along with having Fallon in my arms, feels very different from when I danced with her at her prom.

I know Fallon's responsible for choosing the band and the music they'll perform, and knowing she chose Secrets by One Republic *for the opening song, makes me listen to every word.*

Everyone in the hall fades away, and for the life of me, I can't break eye contact with Fallon. It's like she's placing me under a spell.

The next song, Rewrite The Stars by Zac Efron and Zendaya, *makes my heartbeat speed up, and anticipation begins to hum between our bodies.*

It feels like Fallon's trying to tell me how she feels through the music.

Moving my hand from her hip and up her back, I pull her closer to me until our chests touch.

There's always been a special friendship between us, but right now, it's more – it's filled with the possibility of so much more.

As the song grows with intensity, my lips part, and I watch as emotions play over Fallon's beautiful face.

My heart slams hard against my ribs as Fallon's lips move, and she whispers the final lyrics of the song, 'You know I want you. It's not a secret I try to hide. But I can't have you. We're bound to break, and my hands are tied.'

Chapter 12

FALLON

I'm sitting out back on the veranda, looking at the storm clouds drifting closer.

I hear the door open, and glancing over my shoulder, I watch as Dad comes to take a seat next to me.

We sit in silence for a while, then Dad says, "Before I met your mother, my world felt black and white."

I turn my eyes to him, and when he takes hold of my hand, I struggle to smile.

"I don't think I would've made it through my last year at Trinity without her."

Shock ripples through me from hearing Dad's confession. He's always been the strongest man I know, and to hear that he went through a rough time, makes him look more human in my eyes.

"I wasn't in a good place with your Uncle Julian and grandfather. I only had your Uncle Mason and Uncle Lake to lean on."

I turn my body toward Dad and lean my head against the high back chair. Wrapping both my hands around his, I wait for him to continue.

"But then your Mom burst into my life like a kaleidoscope of color. She changed everything. My relationship with Julian and my father. She... made me stronger."

"And that's why you call her your rainbow," I murmur.

"Yes." Dad nods, then turns his gaze to mine. "I guess what I'm trying to say is that things will get better. They always do."

I suck in a deep breath and lower my eyes to our joined hands. "It doesn't feel like it will get better," I admit. "Things between Kao and me will never be what they were before the accident happened. And the scars..."

I'll never feel like a woman again.

Dad gets up from the chair and comes to crouch in front of me. There's an earnest expression darkening his eyes. "In four weeks, you'll go for the surgery, and Dr. Menard will remove all the scarring. I know it's hard right now, but hold out for one month."

It's taking all my strength just to make it to tomorrow. A month feels like an eternity.

Dad must see the hopelessness on my face because he rises to his feet and pulls me up.

When he frames my face with both hands, the lump in my throat grows impossibly big. The stitches were removed two days ago, but it did nothing to improve the horrible swollen scars.

Dad leans closer, his eyes burning with certainty, and his mouth set in a determined line. "You are so beautiful, Fallon." Then he leans down, and he presses his lips to my right cheek.

I fist my hands at my sides and squeeze my eyes shut as I say, "You're my Dad. You'll always think I'm beautiful."

"You are," I hear Uncle Mason.

Dad moves to the side, and as Uncle Mason and Uncle Lake join us outside, it's so hard not to breakdown and cry.

Uncle Mason's sharp gaze drifts over my face, and then he states with so much certainty I can feel it in my bones, "You are fucking breathtaking. No amount of scarring will ever change that."

When I shake my head, Uncle Mason asks, "Does the scar on my arm make me look any different?"

I shake my head again. "You're a man, Uncle Mace. It makes you look rugged."

"In four weeks, you'll look good as new," Uncle Lake adds his opinion.

I know. But it doesn't make me feel any better.

"What's really the problem?" Uncle Lake asks. He's always been so damn perceptive, just like Jase.

Kao.

With the business ties between our families, I don't want to say something that will cause friction.

Instead of admitting the truth, I say, "I know a month from now everything will be different. It's just hard right now."

My uncles and Dad give me a hug, and then Uncle Lake says, "Come on, I brought food."

His words make the corner of my mouth curve up as I follow them back inside the house.

———————

I've resumed my visits to my grandfather, and sitting on the couch next to him, I wait for him to start the movie we'll be watching.

Since I turned thirteen, watching classic movies have been our thing, where Gramps play chess with Jase. Carla

157

and Gramps read the same books, and with Forest, he plays golf.

When Gramps goes to Youtube instead of selecting a movie, I frown.

"Have patience with me, my girl. I don't go on Youtube often," Gramps explains. "Ahh... there it is."

Then he presses play on a reconstructive video done by Dr. Menard. My eyes are glued to the TV screen as Dr. Menard explains how he did reconstructive surgery on a woman who had suffered domestic violence. Seeing the before and after pictures leave me speechless.

When the video ends, Gramps says, "I wanted you to see how good your doctor is, so you won't have any worries about your impending surgery."

From talking to my family the past weeks and now having watched the video, I do feel confident that Dr. Menard will be able to help me.

"I know he's good," I agree with Gramps. "I'm worried about going back to the academy and having to attend classes for the three weeks before the surgery," I explain.

A dark frown settles between Gramps' heavy eyebrows, and then he barks, "You're my girl, and if anyone gives you any trouble, I'll end them."

My grandfather's fierce protectiveness warms my heart, but it doesn't do anything to lessen my anxiety.

"Tell me what you're worried about," Gramps urges me to open up to him.

Knowing he won't back down, I let out a heavy sigh. "Kao."

The thunderous expression on Gramps' face darkens.

"I'm scared of his reaction. Noah has been sending me updates regarding Kao's vision, and this morning he said Kao could see finer details like faces and what they were wearing." My anxiety has increased with each day closer to the end of the Christmas break. I don't want to go back. I wish I could hide at home until after the surgery, but missing a whole month of school is also not an option. "I don't want Kao to see the scars. It would kill me if he were repulsed by me."

"Are you in a relationship with Kao?" Gramps asks.

I shake my head. "We were close before the accident and were on our first date when it happened."

"And after the accident? How was your relationship with him?"

"He said he wants to be just friends." I suck in a suffocating breath. "After he found out I got hurt, he withdrew from me."

Gramps nods, the corners of his mouth pulling down. "It's simple," he grumbles. "The boy's not worthy of you."

I shake my head, and bringing a hand up, I tuck some hair behind my left ear. "But I love him."

"Even so," Gramps reaches for my hand and gives it a squeeze, "Those who mind don't matter, and those who matter won't mind."

Easier said than done.

"You're right." I force a smile to my face, and getting up, I grab our cups. "I'll make us more coffee while you select the movie."

I try not to hurry to the kitchen because even though my grandfather is right, I can't stop worrying. I wouldn't survive it a second time if Kao were to be repulsed by the scars. I'm barely hanging on as is, and it feels like a feather could knock me over.

God, how am I going to do this? I have to go back in two days.

KAO

There's a constant smile on my face as I sit in the living room. Movement catches my eye, and it widens my smile. I can make out Mom, even though she's blurry, as she walks toward me. Everything is still black and white, but if I focus for an extended period of time, the blurring decreases a little. I can see so much better than a week ago.

Dad almost cried when I recognized him a week ago. Hell, I almost cried. It's been a long three weeks of recovering, and I wouldn't wish it on my worst enemy, but things are starting to look up.

The healing has given me hope. If my eyes keep getting better, there's a chance for Fallon and me. I'll be able to offer her a future again. The thought makes my heartbeat speed up. Not having contact with her the past three weeks has been nothing short of hell. I have to hear how she's doing via Jade, Mila, and Noah.

We're going back to the campus this afternoon so we can get settled in. I'm nervous and worried I've hurt Fallon too much, and any chance I might've had with her is gone.

But I have a plan. First, I'm going to work my ass off to get our friendship back on track. Once my sight is good enough for me to see clearly enough to function on my own, I'll pursue her with everything I have.

With a little luck, we might be together by the end of the month. It's a new year, and I have new hopes.

Becoming independent and getting Fallon back being at the top of the list.

It's getting late, and there's no sign of Fallon and Hana.

"Kao, dinner is here," Noah calls from the kitchen.

It's weird moving around. I thought it would be easier with my sight getting better, but I find myself still counting the paces because I can't see the smaller pieces of furniture.

I walk down the hallway and finding a chair, I'm careful as I sit down. "What are we eating?"

"Cheeseburgers and fries," Noah answers while taking two bottles of water from the fridge. He sets one down in front of me.

"Thanks." Noah's been sticking to burgers because I can make out what I'm eating then. Smaller foods like vegetables and steak, is still a challenge.

While we eat, Noah says, "We need to finish the business plan so I can hand it in tomorrow. You'll be caught up with all the work then."

"Thanks for all the help."

I hear the front door open, and my head immediately snaps in the direction of the sound.

"Hey guys, how was your Christmas break?" Hana asks when she spots us. It sends my heart rate shooting through the ceiling. "Oh, and happy New Year."

When Fallon enters the suite, my heart rate shoots sky-high.

Hana gives each of us a hug, but my eyes are locked on Fallon as she moves closer to Noah. "Good to see you again," she says to him.

I get up and move closer to her. Not knowing what to say, I wrap my right arm around her. She gives me a quick pat on the back then tries to pull away, but I tighten my hold on her while bringing my left arm around her as well. Still at a loss for words, I murmur, "I'm glad you're back."

Holding Fallon, I finally feel like I'm home and not just stumbling through life. I take in a deep breath of her scent, and it feels like I can breathe again. It has me admitting, "I missed you."

Fallon doesn't hug me as tightly, and when she pulls away a second time, I let her go.

"How's your sight?" she asks, and I don't miss the tension in her voice and how she turns her face away from me.

163

"Better. Every day I notice a change."

"That's good to hear." She moves away from me. "I need to unpack. Catch you later."

When the girls have gone to their rooms, Noah mutters, "That wasn't half as bad as I thought it would be."

"Yeah," I agree. "The awkwardness is still there, but at least she didn't slap the shit out of me."

Noah whacks me lightly upside the head. "That's on behalf of Fallon, who's too much of a lady to hit you." We finish our meals, then Noah says, "Time for eyedrops, then we need to hit the business plan hard."

I get up from the stool and ask, "Where do you want to do this?"

"Sit on the couch. I'll get everything. I'm tired of being holed up in your room."

I walk over to the living room and sit down. Noah comes back with everything we'll need, then says, "I've dimmed the lights. You can take off the sunglasses."

Removing them, I set the glasses down on the couch and grin at Noah when I can make eye contact with him.

I hear footsteps coming down the hallway, and glancing in that direction, I see Fallon and Hana come into the open space.

"Hold up," I whisper to Noah, and getting up, I walk toward the girls.

Fallon freezes, and when I get near her, she begins to turn around, but I quickly take hold of her arm, and it makes a surprised gasp burst from her.

I move in front of her and notice her hair is hanging over the right side of her face. I've been worried about her injuries and the surgery she has to go for. When I lift a hand to her face, she tries to pull back, but I tighten my grip on her arm.

"Let me see."

She shakes her head. "I don't want any of you to see." Her voice trembles, and it makes worry explode inside my chest, and a bad feeling ripples over me.

I try to move her hair away, but Fallon rears back and turns her face to the side. "I said no, Kao."

Determined to see how severe her injuries are, I take hold of her face, and then my fingers brush over swollen ridges.

She yanks away again, and it has me snapping, "Hold still, Fallon."

"No!" She manages to pull free and darts back down the hallway. I go after her and grab her arm again before she can reach her room. As she swings toward me, her hair moves, and I can make out dark scarring on the whole right side of her face and neck. I can't see the finer details or coloring, but the fact that I can see the cuts means they're fucking bad.

Horror crashes over me as I realize Fallon got hurt a hell of a lot worse than she let on.

Chapter 13

FALLON

I thought things were bad, but they're nothing compared to the anguish drowning me as Kao's eyes focus on my face.

Maybe he can't see well enough to make out the scars.

My hope is fleeting, and it dies a sudden and awful death as shock tightens his features.

"Christ, Fallon," he gasps. "You said it was nothing to worry about."

A searing pain rips what's left of my world apart.

"Why didn't you tell me the cuts were so bad?" he lashes out at me, his shocked expression quickly turning to horror.

This is the moment I feared most, and it's turning out to be a nightmare. Out of everyone here, why did Kao have to see the scars?

I close my eyes so I won't see his horrorstruck face anymore. Shame begins to burn in my chest, scorching the last of my femininity away.

Self-preservation takes over, and I rip my arm out of Kao's hold. Trying to save whatever's left of my self-esteem, I bite the words out, "Why would I? You decided I wasn't good enough for you any longer the second you found out I got hurt. I didn't think it would change anything between us."

I know my words are cruel, but I can't stop them from falling over my lips.

It's also the truth.

Turning away from Kao, I walk into my room while trying to cover the scars again before anyone else can see them.

"Is that what you think?" Kao asks behind me.

"That's what I know!" I walk to my dressing table. Picking up my brush, I begin to fix my hair.

God, Kao's hand brushed over the scars.

The thought alone is enough to make my stomach roll with nausea.

"Fallon," Kao begins to talk, his voice softer.

Mortified and crushed, I swing back to him and scream, "Get out of my room! I'm done talking about it." My breaths explode over my lips, and I'm a second away from losing my composure. When Kao doesn't move, I dart forward and shove at his chest. "Get out! Get out! Get out!"

168

Jase and Hana come into the room, and luckily Hana pulls Kao away.

Jase quickly shuts the door then rushes over to me. "What happened?" He begins to lift his hands, but when I shake my head, still trying to breathe through the gut-wrenching heartbreak, Jase stills, and his eyes lock on my face.

God. I can't.

Shock ripples over Jase's features, and the blow slams my feet from under me. I crumble to the floor as a cry tears out of me.

Hunter bursts into the room just as Jase kneels down in front of me. I try to gasp for air, but another cry completely robs me of my breath.

I can't.

I wish I could just disappear. I wish I never existed.

Jase frames my face with both his hands, and he leans in close. "Shh… it's okay. Breathe, Fallon."

I try to shake my head as I gasp for air but my neck cramps up, and it feels like my lungs have collapsed along with the last of my will to live.

Hunter's arm comes around my shoulders. "Come on, Fallon. Just breathe."

I shake my head again, unable to think straight.

Hana comes running into the room and pushes her way through Jase and Hunter. The moment my feverish eyes land on her, my body shoots forward and into the safety of her arms. My arms wrap tightly around her, and I bury my face against her neck as I cry for everything I've lost.

Oh, God, why did I survive? I would've been better off dead.

"Guys, you can leave," Hana snaps. "I've got this."

"But…" Jase begins to argue.

"Leave so I can calm her down!" Hana yells.

Oh, God, make it stop.

I manage to draw in a strangled breath before another cry tears out of my burning chest.

Hana holds me, and she begins to murmur, "Everyone's gone. It's just us. I've got you." She presses a kiss to my scarred cheek, and sobs wrack my body. "Shh… I've got you." I hear her voice tremble and know she's close to tears as well.

I swallow a couple of times and focus on getting air into my lungs, and then another wave of unrelenting devastation hits. "Kao… touched the… scars," I stutter through my tears.

Hana pushes me a little back and says, "Don't worry about it right now. Just breathe with me." I begin to shake

170

my head, but Hana quickly frames my face, and her gaze locks with mine. "Look at me, Fallon." The expression on her face is filled with all the love she feels for me, and it lends my broken heart and defeated spirit strength. "I love you. You're my best friend, my sister. I love you so much."

Her words help calm me down until I'm able to breathe normally again.

A caring smile softens her features. "I love you more than anything in this world. You're the most important person in my life."

Moving forward, I wrap my arms around her again and hold onto her for dear life. "I love you too."

After a couple of seconds, Hana pulls back again. "The scars don't change who you are. You're strong, and you have an unbreakable spirit. Okay? You just lost control for a little while, but you'll get back up again. And you'll be so much stronger."

I nod because what Hana says is the truth. I can't stay down forever. My social standing doesn't allow for people like me to give up.

"You're allowed to hurt," Hana keeps going. "You're allowed to break, and I promise I'll be there to pick up every piece and to help put you back together. But after you've reached rock bottom, there's only one way, and that's up." Hana climbs to her feet, and then she pulls me up. Her expression is fierce and loyal as she stares at me. "And by God, we'll keep getting up no matter what comes our way. Okay?"

I nod again. "Yes."

"I want to hear you say it," she demands.

"We'll keep getting up no matter what comes our way," I repeat her words.

Her face softens, and she uses her thumbs to wipe the tears from my cheeks. "Do you feel better?"

I've hardly managed to calm down, and then the wave of devastation washes over me again. "Kao saw the scars." I swallow hard. "Jase and Hunter as well."

"Do you trust me?" she asks.

I nod. There's no one I trust more than Hana.

I watch as she goes to open the door, and then Jase bursts into the room. He walks right up to me and locks me against his chest. When he presses a kiss to my cheek and then my temple, my body jerks in his hold. Pulling back, he frames my face, and his eyes burn in mine. "I don't care what you look like, Fallon."

My chin begins to tremble, but I swallow hard on the tears.

"I wish you didn't hide that you weren't coping from me," Jase continues.

Hunter brushes a hand up and down my back. "We're a family. Why didn't you tell us?"

Because you were all busy being there for Kao.

Hana steps closer, and there's a bite to her tone as she says, "You were all a little busy."

I see the guilt ripple over Jase and Hunter's faces, and it only makes me feel like shit.

"I still need to unpack and shower," I murmur, too tired to hash things out with them.

"Have you had dinner?" Hunter asks. "I can order something for you."

I don't have any appetite. "I'm good."

"Can I make you some coffee?" Jase asks, and it makes the corner of my mouth lift. He doesn't make coffee for anyone.

"Yeah, I'd like to taste your coffee," I tease.

A grin forms on my cousin's face. "I keep my special talents hidden, or everyone would have me making coffee all the time."

I let out a chuckle. "Yeah, keep lying to yourself."

The banter helps ease the tension, and once Jase and Hunter have left, I turn to my luggage.

"Go shower," Hana orders. "I'll unpack for you."

"My mother hen," I say, giving her another hug. "I wouldn't be able to survive without you."

KAO

I'm so fucking shocked, I don't even take in that Noah's put in my eyedrops and placed my sunglasses back on my face.

My body trembles from the heartache and regret building in me. I should've been there for Fallon. If I hadn't pushed her away because of my own insecurities and worry, I would've known how much she was struggling.

God, I failed her in the worst way possible.

How will I ever make this up to her? Can I even?

Hearing her cry and knowing I'm the last person she wants near her ripped my heart out of my chest.

The woman I love with everything I am broke down in front of me, and there was nothing I could do. It tightens my chest until it feels like my heart is being squashed into a painful lump.

I take deep breaths, trying to calm down because I need to be strong for Fallon now.

I realize, even though I tried to push Fallon away to protect her from my blindness, my heart never let go of her. She has always been and always will be my life.

I treated Fallon like shit.

God, I wish I could punch myself.

The thoughts make every muscle in my body tense.

Jase comes to sit on the other couch, and Hunter drops down next to him.

"Fuck," Jase mutters, sounding pissed off. "How did we not know?"

"We were all focused on Kao," Noah mutters.

I shut my eyes against the truth. I lost my shit, and our friends scurried to help me. I left Fallon vulnerable.

Fuck, I'm such a weak sack of shit.

"We need to get her through this," Hunter states the obvious.

"Yeah, definitely," Jase says. "Then again, I think Kao's the only one who can help her." My head snaps up, and I look at Jase. "You broke her, so you need to fucking fix her." I can hear the bitter bite in his voice.

I can't argue with the truth.

Nodding, I say, "I wish I knew what to do."

"You fucking man up. When she pushes you away, you fight harder to stay by her side. When she lashes out at you, you fucking take it," Jase says.

Like he did with Mila.

"And I don't want to hear shit about you just being friends with her. We all fucking know you love her," Jase adds.

I begin to get up, but then he snaps, "Not tonight. Give her time to calm down first."

"Also," Hunter adds, "I think Hana will kick your ass if you go near Fallon now."

Jase lets out a tired chuckle. "Who knew Hana could get so angry?"

"Right?" Hunter lets out a sigh. "Fuck, I feel like shit. Fallon has always been there for all of us."

"Yeah, we fucked up badly," Jase mutters.

Me, most of all.

Tonight was one hell of an eye-opener. Fuck waiting for my vision to return completely. Fuck everything but Fallon.

She's all that matters now, and I can only pray I'm not too late.

I'm up at the crack of dawn, and after getting dressed, I slowly make my way down the hallway. When I walk into the kitchen and I see Fallon preparing a cup of coffee, I pause.

All I want to do is wrap her up in my arms and kiss everything better, but I know it won't be that easy.

First things first.

I move closer, and Fallon turns toward me. The second she sees me, she drops the full cup of coffee in the sink and darts around the other side of the table. I move as quickly as I can to my left and block her way to the hallway.

I can feel the tension coming off her, and not wanting a repeat of last night, I say, "Remember what I said about us being just friends?"

"Yeah, it's kind of hard to forget," she bites the words out.

"I lied." I wish I could make the past four weeks disappear.

Fallon shakes her head. "I don't need your pity." She darts past me, and I almost go after her, but when I see

Hana waiting at the end of the hall for Fallon, I rethink myself.

Fuck, this is going to be so much harder than I thought it would be.

Fallon believed the lie I spewed, but she won't spare a minute for the truth, and it's so unlike her. Just another sign telling me how much she's hurting.

I make three cups of coffee, and praying I don't spill half of it, I carry two cups to Fallon's room. "Hana," I call by the closed door.

When she opens, I hold the two cups out to her. "I know it's a shitty peace offering, but…"

"It's a start," Hana sasses me. "Keep making us coffee until you graduate, and we can talk again."

I let out a chuckle. "Deal." When she takes the coffee from me, I add, "Tell her I meant what I said."

"Just give her time," Hana whispers.

I nod and take a step backward. "She can have all the time she needs, but I'm done running away."

"That's good to hear. I really didn't want to beat you up," Hana admits, and it draws another chuckle from me.

"I'm glad she has you," I say before I walk back to the kitchen to have my own coffee.

Chapter 14

FALLON

I tried to cover the scarring as much as I could, but the more foundation I put on, the worse it looked. Feeling hopeless, I wrap a scarf around my neck to keep my hair in place because I'll die if I have to suffer through a repeat of last night. I hardly slept, too worried about starting classes today.

My thoughts are also filled with what Kao said earlier in the kitchen.

He lied?

Ha.

I still remember clearly how he shot me down and said we're nothing more than friends. I'm filled with guilt for the part I played in our accident, and nothing he says will make me forget that he also blames me. Rightly so, as well.

I let out an exhausted sigh. It's only eight in the morning, and I'm already tired and emotionally drained.

'I lied.'

Kao's words echo through me again, but then I see the look on his face when he saw the scars. The shock and horror.

I don't want his pity. It's up there with the disgust I saw written all over his face.

My eyes dart to the mirror and flit over my appearance. Where I used to spend hours getting ready and loving every minute of it, I now rush through a quick routine. The less I look at myself, the better.

Still reeling from the devastating blow I took last night, I can't bring myself to leave my room. I only went to make myself coffee earlier because I thought everyone would still be asleep. But now that my friends are all up and getting ready for the day, I'm apprehensive about facing them.

There's a soft tap on my door, and I can't force the words for whoever it is to enter. The door slowly opens, and then Mila peeks in, and when she sees me standing in the middle of the room, she lets herself in. "Hey," she whispers as she shuts the door. Then she seems to hesitate. "I'm sorry, Fallon."

A light frown forms on my forehead.

"I've been a shitty friend to you. I should've known you weren't okay." Mila takes a couple of steps closer to me, and I see the regret on her face. "I'm sorry I wasn't there for you."

"There's nothing to be sorry for. I'm fine," I lie, not wanting to upset Mila. She's been through enough, and the last thing I want is for her to be sucked into my nightmare.

Mila's gaze locks with mine, and then she shakes her head. "What happened to me was different, but... I felt tainted... ugly."

I drop my eyes from hers.

"I felt like I'd never be whole again," Mila continues.

I wrap my arms around my waist as her words echo exactly what I feel.

"But I was wrong." Mila comes to stand right in front of me. "It's taking a lot of time, but piece by piece, I'm healing."

I shake my head and repulsed by myself, I whisper, "You're stronger than me."

"No," Mila shakes her head, and the corner of her mouth lifts, "that's where you're wrong. You're so much stronger than me."

I squeeze my eyes shut and take a step back from her. I need space to breathe.

"I had Jase. He kept me standing, and you all stood by me, as well." Mila begins to reach for my arm but stops.

181

"Kao couldn't be there for you because he got hurt as well, and we were all so worried about his blindness that we… we forgot about you. It's been a month, and you're still standing. You did that on your own, and I'm so sorry."

"It's okay," I murmur.

"I'm here now, and Jade is waiting so we can go to class. She'll punch anyone who dares to look at you."

My eyes dart up to Mila's, and it has her admitting, "I know how daunting the first couple of weeks can be. People are going to gossip, but don't listen to them. Their opinions don't matter."

Hana and I don't have the same class schedule because she's studying law, where I'm doing my MBA. I was worried about walking around the campus by myself. For the first time in a long while, I feel a sense of relief, knowing Mila and Jade will be with me.

"How did you deal with people staring and talking?" I ask.

"I didn't," Mila confesses. "It almost broke me until I realized they really didn't matter. Just keep telling yourself that."

'Those who mind don't matter, and those who matter don't mind.'

Mila takes a step closer to me, a tentative smile on her face. "Are we good?"

My lips curve easily as I nod. I close the distance between us, and we hug for a moment. Then Mila whispers, "I love you, and I'm here for you every step of the way."

It means a lot to me that she came to talk with me.

Together we leave my room and find Jade and Hana waiting in the living room.

"I don't have class until ten, so I can walk with you," Hana offers.

"Take the morning off," I tease her. "I'll have Mila and Jade with me."

Jade gets up from the couch. "Just say the word, and I'll punch anyone for you." Then she grins at me.

"I might take you up on that," I joke.

I'm still apprehensive as we walk to the front door, knowing there's only so much the girls can protect me from.

"Hold up," I hear Jase call and when he comes to take my bag from me. "We're sticking with you for the first couple of days." Hunter comes jogging up the hallway. And just like that, I have an entourage.

Leaving the suite surrounded by my friends helps more than I thought it would. I hide between them, and luckily, no one dares to approach me with Jase and Jade looking like they're ready to go to war for me.

KAO

When everyone left with Fallon, the frustration rolled back in because she doesn't want me near her.

"Come on, let's go," Noah says.

I let out a sigh as I get up, and we walk out of the suite. Even though I won't be able to take down notes from the classes, I can sit in on them and listen, which will help a lot. Besides, the sooner I get back into our regular routine, the better for everyone.

When we walk out of the building, the extra dark sunglasses help against the sunlight. Noah always makes sure I don't forget them. He's been such an amazing pillar of strength, and a hundred lifetimes won't be enough to repay him for everything he's done for me.

"Hey guys," Nate, a junior, greets us. "Sorry to hear about the accident, Kao."

I nod, feeling uncomfortable. I never know how to reply when people say they're sorry. It's not like it's their fault.

"Let me know if I can help with anything," Nate offers.

"Thanks," I reply before we keep walking.

Entering our first class, Noah picks seats in the back where it's a little darker. "I never noticed the back being so dark, or I would've hidden out here and snoozed through the lectures," I joke as we sit down.

"Jase had them remove the fluorescent lights in the back for you," Noah informs me.

Surprised, I ask, "Seriously?"

"Yeah. Remember to thank him."

"Of course."

The day goes by slow and at least not too many students come up to me. Then again, I've always been an introvert and never encouraged them to interact with me before the accident happened, so I don't see why they would change toward me now.

But Fallon's always been an extrovert. Will today be different for her? God, I hope she isn't swamped with people.

"Can you check with one of the girls and see how Fallon's day was?" I ask Noah.

"Sure." He makes the call, then says, "Fallon's okay. They're heading to the restaurant. Are we going to join them for an early dinner?"

"Yeah, let's go," I agree, hoping it will help if Fallon and I are thrown together in a social setting.

When we walk into the restaurant, and I see that everyone's in their usual seats, a smile begins to curve around my lips. I sit down next to Fallon, and immediately, her hand flies up to make sure her hair is covering her face.

Placing my hand on the back of her neck, I lean in and press a kiss to the side of her head. Fallon jerks, and when I pull back, she turns her face to me and whispers, "Don't do that."

"Why?" I ask, working hard to keep the smile on my face so she won't see the worry I feel for her.

"You're the one who broke things off between us," she mutters under her breath so the others won't hear.

"I didn't mean it," I reply. Needing to make her understand why I said those things to her, I ask, "Can we talk after dinner so I can explain myself?"

Fallon picks up her glass of coke and takes a sip, then says, "Like you said, it's not like we were in a relationship, to begin with, so you don't have to explain anything."

I was prepared for this because Fallon doesn't give her trust easily, and I hurt her in the worst way when she needed me most. It will take a lot of time and hard work, and I have no intention of giving up.

Leaning back into her, my mouth brushes over the hair covering her ear. "Take all the time you need, but I'm not backing down. I hurt you, and I understand I'll have to prove myself to you again."

Fallon lowers her head, and I hear her suck in a trembling breath, and then she whispers, "Stop. Please."

Not wanting to push her too hard, I pull back and ask, "Have you all placed your orders?"

"Yeah," Jade answers.

"What are you in the mood for?" Noah asks me.

"Steak, please." Then I joke with him, "I've had my fill of burgers."

Noah signals a waiter for us and places our order.

Looking in Jase's direction, I say, "Thanks for taking care of the lights in the lecture halls."

"Sure." Then Jase mentions, "We should have a movie night after dinner."

Before any of us can answer, Summer taps Fallon on the shoulder and says, "Hey, Fallon. We need to meet for the Valentines' Ball. When's a good day for you?"

Fallon shakes her head. "I'm no longer on the decorating committee. You can take charge and arrange everything."

I glance at Fallon as a shocked silence follows her words.

"Uhm... are you sure?" Summer asks, probably not wanting to step on anyone's toes.

"Yeah," Fallon states. "I'm too busy now."

"Oh... okay."

When Summer leaves, Hana says, "But you love being on the committee."

"I need to focus on my school work and get my grades back up," is all Fallon offers as an explanation.

"I can help if you've fallen behind," Noah offers.

"I'm good. Thanks, Noah," Fallon replies, her voice sounding warmer.

"Kao, your average must've shot through the roof with Noah doing all your work," Jase jokes.

I grin at Jase. "The perks of having a genius for a best friend."

Our food comes, and while eating, my thoughts are consumed with Fallon. I try to think of grand gestures to sweep her off her feet, but every idea I come up with is instantly dismissed. I can't drive, and I seriously don't think we're ready to get in the same car after the accident.

Deciding to just pick up where we left off before the shit hit the fan, I can only hope that my actions will win her over.

Chapter 15

FALLON

Besides being super aware of the scars, today wasn't as bad as I thought it would be. No one approached me, and having my friends around me helped a lot.

Dinner was awkward, especially when Kao pretended like nothing had happened between us. I have no idea why he's trying to pick up where we left of. I can't just forget that he broke my heart.

'Just friends, Fallon... Nothing more... It's not like we dated... We weren't in a relationship... We're just going back to the way things were.'

Is that what Kao is trying to do? Save our friendship?

I shake my head because there's no way I can pretend everything is fine and just be friends with him.

"Guys, what movie are we watching?" Jase yells from the living room.

I let out a sigh. I wish I could climb in bed but not wanting to upset my friends more than I already have, I take a deep breath and then leave the safety of my room.

When I walk into the shared space, I notice all the snacks and drinks piled on the coffee table.

Usually, I'd spread a blanket over the carpet so Kao and I can lie down. My heart mourns the loss of the special little things I used to share with him.

Jase and Mila are already comfortable on the one couch, and Jade and Hunter are on the other, leaving the three-seater couch open.

Wanting to see where everyone sits, I first go to the fridge and take out a bottle of water. While I slowly sip on the cool liquid, Hana comes down the hallway, dressed in a pair of jeans and a pretty pale pink blouse.

"Tristan called. He's picking me up," she explains her attire. "I'll have to skip movie night."

"Are the two of you dating?" Jade asks.

"Yeah, I guess so. We haven't spoken about making it official yet," Hana answers. She comes to give me a hug, then asks, "Will you be okay?"

"Sure," I grin at my friend. "Enjoy your date."

I'm happy things are starting to get serious between Hana and Tristan. My friend deserves a good man.

191

After Hana leaves, Kao and Noah take a seat on the last open couch, and I'm fresh out of luck when I have no choice but to sit next to Kao. I was hoping Noah would sit in the middle

Not wanting to make a scene, I lift my chin and go sit down. I press close to the armrest, leaving an open gap between Kao and me.

"What are we watching?" Noah asks.

"Fantastic Beasts," Mila answers as she presses play on the movie.

At least my left side is facing Kao, and I don't have to worry about the scars being visible. Pulling my legs up, I curl into the armrest, and I use my right arm to rest my head on.

I only manage to keep my eyes open for the first twenty minutes of the movie. The last thing I remember is seeing a platypus stealing stuff.

A rocking motion draws me out of my sleep, and it takes a couple of seconds for the realization to sink in that someone's carrying me. Lifting my head, I mutter, "Is the movie over?"

"Yeah," I hear Kao answer, and it clears the last of the sleep from my head.

My eyes pop open and come face to face with Kao's strong jawline. Feeling awkward, the words rush from me, "Put me down."

Kao ignores me, and it doesn't help I make any further fuss because he turns into my room. When he sets me down on the bed, I quickly move to the side and get up.

"Please, can we talk?" Kao asks, and then he takes a seat on the edge of the bed. When he looks up, I feel the intensity of his eyes settling on me. It's just as powerful as it's always been, making my insides hum with awareness.

Knowing I can't avoid him forever, I go sit on the stool by my dresser. My hand flutters self-consciously over my hair, making sure the scars are still covered.

"I'm sorry, Fallon," Kao murmurs.

I lift my eyes to his and whisper, "It is what it is. Let's just forget everything and move forward."

Kao shakes his head. "I don't want to forget, and there's no moving forward without you."

"It's going to take me a while before I can be friends with you again," I admit. If I ever manage to get to that point.

"I don't want that either," Kao says.

A frown begins to form on my forehead, and even though he hurt me, I still want him in my life. It pains me to

193

say, "Then I guess the least we can do is to be civil with each other for the –"

"I want you," Kao interrupts me.

I close my eyes against the mixture of pain and hope his words cause me.

Why now?

It's been a month since everything went to hell. He pushed me away. He treated me like crap. I'll never forget his anger and revulsion.

But I still love him.

"I want to be with you," Kao repeats himself.

When I shake my head, my hand instantly flies up to make sure the hair didn't move away from my cheek.

Kao gets up and walks toward me. When he crouches in front of me, he places a hand on my knee.

"I lied when I said I only cared for you as a friend. I was scared I wouldn't see again, and I didn't want to tie you down to a blind man who can't offer you anything."

His confession rips the air from my lungs, and too scared to let the hope fully back in, I can only stare at him.

"I love you, Fallon."

Hearing the words for the first time is bittersweet. It's all I ever wanted, but now it's overshadowed by the trauma we suffered.

"Not as a friend but as a man," Kao continues. "One who fucked up badly. I can only hope with time you'll forgive me and give me another chance."

"You hurt me," I whisper, the wounds his words and actions have caused over the past weeks still raw.

"I'm sorry. I wish I could go back and do things differently." My eyes flit over his face, looking for any sign of pity. "I love you," he says again.

This is not how I wanted to hear those words. Not when everything is broken.

"It felt like you died," I admit, wanting him to know how much he has hurt me. "I can't just pick up where we left off. Too much has happened."

"I understand," he immediately agrees. "As long as you'll give me a chance to show you, I'm still the same man I was before the accident."

I suck in a trembling breath. "That's the problem, Kao." A frown begins to form between his brows, and it has me continuing, "The instant life got difficult, you left me. I understand the blindness was a huge shock and adjustment, but you pushed me away. Harshly. You took all your anger out on everyone around you. When I told you about my injuries, you shoved me aside with disgust." I'm unable to continue as the tears threaten to fall. I take a moment to swallow them back and breathe through the heartache. "You hugged Mila, but you wouldn't let me near you." I suck in another trembling breath, then whimper, "It hurts too much."

Kao rises to his feet, and taking hold of my shoulders, he pulls me up. When his arms wrap around me, I have zero strength to push him away.

KAO

Hearing how much I've hurt Fallon is hard. Needing to comfort her, I pull her against my chest and hold her tightly.

I press a kiss to the top of her head and say, "I was nothing short of an asshole. I'm so sorry. I wish I could turn back time and do things differently." I press another kiss to her hair, then murmur, "One of the reasons I pushed you away was because I wanted to save you from being tied down by a blind man."

Fallon pulls back and turns her face up to me. "What are the other reasons?"

"Because I hurt you," I admit. "I can't remember the accident, but I was the one driving. You got hurt when I should've kept you safe."

Fallon just stares at me for a while, then she asks, "You can't remember?"

Shaking my head, I explain, "The last thing I can recall clearly is us having lunch at the restaurant. There are jumbled pieces of getting ready for the date, but I don't remember getting in the car or driving."

"It wasn't your fault," Fallon states. "You turned my side of the car away from the truck and pinned me to the seat with your arm. You did everything you could."

Hearing the words from Fallon makes me feel a hell of a lot better.

Then Fallon murmurs, "I told you to take that route." She takes a shaky breath. "It was my fault."

Frowning at her, I shake my head. "No, Fallon. It's definitely not your fault."

"You said we should never have been on that road, to begin with," Fallon argues.

God, I wish I had never said that. I didn't know we took Fallon's route.

"I didn't mean anything I said that day, Fallon. It was all lies. I wanted you to forget about me and to move on with your life."

Fallon's gaze burns on me as she asks, "Did you really think I'd move on?" She lets out an empty sounding chuckle. "Because then you don't know me at all."

"I wanted to spare you future heartache," I try my best to explain.

Fallon moves around me and goes to sit on the bed. "Even if you had remained blind, even if your vision doesn't fully return, I would've stood happily by your side, Kao. That's what it means to love someone unconditionally. I wanted to be the one to help and comfort you." She takes a couple of deep breaths, and I can hear the ache in her voice as she continues, "You didn't spare me from any heartache."

"I was… God, I was stupid, Fallon. I was caught up in my anger. I wasn't myself." I don't know how else to explain the dark place I was stuck in.

"I saw the revulsion on your face," she whispers, her voice tight. "And I don't blame you." She lets out a painful burst of laughter. "God, right before the accident, we were joking about you being the beauty and me being the beast in our relationship." Her voice hitches.

Darting forward, I sit down beside her and pull her into an embrace. "Don't say that."

Fallon yanks back. "But it's the truth!" She gasps for air. "I look like a monster, Kao!"

Determined to show her the scars don't matter, I frame her face with both my hands and lean into her. "You can never be a monster." She tries to pull back again, but it has me snapping, "I don't care about the scars, Fallon! I love you, not because of how fucking gorgeous you are, but because of how priceless you are. Your strength is unbelievable. You are compassionate, loyal, and you never back down from anything." Wanting to show her that I mean every word, I close the distance between us and press my mouth to her quivering lips.

This is not how I wanted our first kiss to happen. I wanted to make the anticipation build. But that doesn't matter anymore because as Fallon gasps, I tilt my head and move my lips against hers. She lifts her hands and takes hold of my forearms, and when she doesn't push me away, I slip my tongue into her mouth.

Awareness of the incredible woman Fallon is, fills every inch of my heart. When my tongue brushes against hers, I can only hear my thundering heartbeat.

God, this woman is my everything.

My mouth caresses hers tenderly, my lips and tongue drinking in the intoxicating taste of her. I pour my love into the kiss, and before I lose control, I manage to pull back.

I wish I could see the color of her eyes right now.

"I don't want to lose you, Fallon. I love you with every inch of my being," I murmur, praying to all that's holy she'll give me a chance.

Her breaths rush over her lips, and she takes a couple of seconds to gather herself, then she whispers, "I need time."

"Anything for you."

"We..." She clears her throat, "We can be friends."

God, no.

The ground rips open beneath me, but then Fallon continues, "Let's first get comfortable being around each other again, and then we can talk about whether we can have a relationship."

Too scared to hope, I ask, "So there's still a chance for us to be together?"

Fallon pulls my hands away from her face, and it's only then that it sinks in, I've been touching her scars without her freaking out. I stare at her face, and I'm able to make out the bumps and swells I felt. The cuts are haphazard over her cheek and neck, but it does nothing to dim her beauty.

"Let's see what happens," she murmurs.

At least it's not a no.

"I can work with that," I reply, a grin tugging at my lips.

Fallon lifts her hand to my face, and her fingers brush over the corner of my mouth. "I missed seeing you smile."

My lips curve against her fingertips. "I missed seeing you."

She drops her hand and asks, "What can you see?"

"Everything's still blurry and black and white, but I can see details like faces, clothing, a cup."

"So, no color?" Fallon asks.

"Not yet. Dr. Hodgson, my ophthalmologist, said it might take another two to three weeks before I can make out the finer details and see color. It differs from person to person."

"So… uhm," she wets her lips nervously. "How much of… the scars did you see?"

"Enough to know it's not a minor injury," I admit. When Fallon remains silent, I ask, "What did your doctor say? Can he help?"

Fallon nods. "My surgery is scheduled for the twenty-fourth. Dr. Menard said he'll be able to reduce it significantly, but there might be white marks once it's healed completely."

"That's good, right?" I ask, glad we're finally talking. I'm taking it as a huge win.

"Yeah," Fallon agrees. "But I still have to walk around like this for three weeks. I don't want anyone to see it."

I lift my hand to her right cheek, but this time, Fallon scoots back. "I don't want you touching it, Kao. Please."

"The scars don't make a difference how I feel about you," I assure her.

Fallon gets up. "Still, I'm not comfortable."

I'm starting to catch on that it's hard for Fallon to say the word scars.

I stand up and murmur, "You'll always be beautiful to me."

She lets out a soft chuckle, and the heartbreak and hopelessness still shimmer through.

"Do you want to sleep, or can I talk you into having a cup of coffee with me?" I ask, wanting to spend more time with her.

"Coffee sounds good."

A smile tugs at my lips.

Fallon's gaze settles on me, and she asks, "You're okay with lights, right?"

"Yeah, mostly. Sometimes my eyes are sensitive, but then I'll just wear the sunglasses indoors, as well."

"Anything else?"

"I'm not allowed to rub my eyes, and I have to sleep with eye shields on. Noah takes care of putting in the eyedrops."

"He's been amazing," she states.

"Yeah, I'm lucky to have him." I take a step toward the door. "Thank you for giving me a chance to explain myself."

"I'm sorry I didn't listen sooner."

She lifts her right hand and begins to pat over her hair. Bringing my arm up, I stop her nervous movements. "I wish you wouldn't hide your face from me." Placing my hand on her lower back, I give her a nudge. "Lead the way."

Fallon doesn't respond to what I said but instead walks out of the room. The instant we step into the hallway, Jase pushes away from where he was leaning against the wall outside Fallon's room. "Night, guys."

"Night." Fallon lets out a real chuckle this time.

He was probably waiting to kick my ass if I screwed things up with Fallon again. Damn, I'd let him.

From this moment on, I'll do everything in my power to make Fallon happy. I'll be the man she deserves.

Chapter 16

FALLON

I make coffee while Kao sits at the table.

So much happened tonight, I'm struggling to process it all.

Kao kissed me.

While I wait for the coffee pot to fill, I lift my fingers to my lips. Feeling his mouth on mine was everything and so much more than I ever thought it would be. Even though I was caught off guard, I don't regret it happening.

I was honest when I told Kao we should first get back to being friends before we can even think of having a relationship.

I'm also hoping to have the surgery before his vision fully returns.

Deep in thought, my fingers slowly move to my cheek, and I feel the roughly raised skin. Knowing Kao touched it makes my stomach lurch.

I yank my hand away and quickly shift my hair back into place.

"What's wrong?" Kao asks.

"Nothing." The word bursts from me. I quickly pour the warm liquid into the cups, then add cream and sugar.

Turning to Kao, I place a cup in front of him.

Kao lets out a chuckle. "I've missed your coffee."

The corner of my mouth lifts a little, and then I say, "I've watched Noah help you. He should've studied medicine."

"Yeah, but you can always take over." It sounds like Kao is teasing me, but I can't be sure. "I sure as hell wouldn't mind you dressing me."

I let out a burst of laughter. "Oh, is that so?"

I sit down next to him and sip on my coffee.

I watch as Kao carefully lifts the cup to his mouth.

"How are you coping?" I ask, wanting to know how he's doing emotionally.

"Better." He sets the cup down, then turns his eyes to me, and instantly I feel overly self-conscious. "Much better now that we've talked."

"Yeah, me too." It has helped to clear the air between us. I hated walking on eggshells around Kao. I feel we've taken a step in the right direction, and it's taken some of the pressure off my shoulders.

I still have one question to ask, but I bite my bottom lip. It might be too soon to open that box of worms. Knowing it won't stop bothering me, I push through and ask, "Why did you refuse the transplant?"

Kao's eyes flit to my face before he lowers them again. He seems to think about his answer, and it makes the corner of my mouth lift. Seeing his trademark habits brings warmth to my chest.

Kao clears his throat, and his features tense. "I wanted to punish myself."

Shocked, I gasp, "Why?"

"Because you got hurt." His eyes lock on mine. "You could've died in the accident, and I just... the guilt drove me insane."

Knowing Kao pushed me away because of his own guilt and heartache makes me regret not fighting harder for him.

"I'm sorry I gave up so quickly," I whisper.

Kao turns his body toward me and holds his hand out to me. "Let's make a deal." When I place my hand in his, he says, "No more sorries. It was a hard month for both of us. Let's focus on the future now."

I nod and say, "Okay."

Letting go of me, Kao places his hand on his thigh. He rests his right elbow on the counter and leans his chin on his knuckles. The pose makes him look strong… and mouthwateringly attractive.

For a moment, it feels like no time has passed at all and that we're right back to how things were between us before the accident ripped us apart.

"Sorry to interrupt, guys," Noah says, popping the bubble I got caught in. "Time for eyedrops."

I watch as Noah sets three bottles on the table, then my gaze goes back to Kao's eyes. I drink in the sight of his striking blue irises, but then a frown begins to form on my forehead, and I lean closer.

Oh my god.

I climb off the stool, and framing Kao's jaw, I lift his face so I can see the stitches around his irises better. "Do the stitches hurt?"

"Not as much as they used to. It comes and goes," Kao replies.

"How will they come out?" I ask, worried that he'll have to undergo another surgery.

"They'll remove them bit by bit as he heals. The whole process can take nine months to a year and a half," Noah informs me.

I let go of Kao and stand back so Noah can administer the drops. I watch closely what he does so I can help out in the future.

Noah picks up on the fact I'm taking in what he does, and he explains, "You have to wait a couple of minutes between the different eye drops."

"Why?" I move a little closer, and seeing how red Kao's eyes are, makes me wish I could do something to make this process easier for him.

"It irritates his eyes."

I nod, and when some of the solution runs down Kao's temple, I quickly reach up and brush the drop away with my thumb.

"Careful," Kao murmurs. "I'll get used to all the attention."

Noah lets out a chuckle, and then he administers the next set of eyedrops. I pick up a bottle and ask, "What are they all for?"

"That one is so Kao's body won't reject the donor cornea."

I glance at Noah. "I was telling Kao, you should've become a doctor like your mother."

"I don't have her patience," he chuckles.

"Could've fooled me," I tease.

Noah gathers the three bottles of eyedrops. "They're just to help with the healing." Then he looks at Kao. "Don't forget to put on the eye shields when you go to bed."

"Are you turning in for the night?" Kao asks.

"Yeah, taking care of your stubborn ass is tiring," he jokes.

Smiling at Noah, I say, "Night."

When Noah disappears down the hallway, I turn my gaze back to Kao. "Do your eyes feel better after the drops?"

"Yeah, they aren't as scratchy then." A mischievous grin spreads over his face. "Looks like it's just us."

I glance at the time, and seeing it's already midnight, my eyes widen. "Damn, we should actually head to bed, or we're totally going to oversleep tomorrow."

Kao begins to get up, and it has me saying, "Wait a sec. Let me just rinse the cups, then I'll help."

I quickly clean up after us, then walk to Kao. "Let's go."

As we walk down the hallway, he says, "Thank you for tonight."

Entering his room, I switch on the light but then pause. "Should I leave the lights off?"

"No, leave them on."

I walk to his bed and pull the covers back. Noticing the eye shields on the bedside table, I ask, "Do you need help putting on the eye shields?"

"In a minute." Kao first makes his way to the bathroom. "Can you help me with the toothbrush and paste?"

"Sure." I dart forward and go stand next to him. I reach for the toothbrush and squirt some paste on, then place it in his hand.

I fill the glass with water and wait until Kao's finished, then hand it to him. I quickly rinse the bristles before placing the toothbrush back in the holder.

Getting a taste of how much help Kao still needs is an eye-opener. I wish I could've helped him sooner.

I follow him back into the bedroom, and instead of getting in bed, he turns to face me. "I really want to hug you right now."

I hesitate for a moment, but not wanting to ruin the ground we've gained, I move forward and wrap my arms around his waist. I press my right cheek to his shirt, and when his arms lock me to him, everything feels right again.

KAO

Actually, I want to drag Fallon into bed with me and hold her all night long. But knowing I can't rush things with her, I force my arms to let go of her.

I sit down on the side of the bed, and again a smile plays around my lips as Fallon carefully helps me put on the eye shields. Even though I can do some of the things myself, I'm holding back so Fallon can help me because I know how important it is to her.

I let out a chuckle and try to joke, "I probably look like a fly now."

"Never," Fallon whispers, and when I lie down, her hair falls over me, she presses a kiss to my cheek. "Night, Kao."

She has such a nurturing soul, it's one of the things I love most about her.

"Night," I murmur. It takes all my strength to lie still and to not beg her to stay.

She turns off the light and then pulls the door shut behind her, and I'm left with my thoughts.

I replay the night's events and remembering everything Fallon said fills me with worry. Her self-esteem took one hell of a knock, and I only helped crush it.

Seeing the consequences of my destructive breakdown makes regret taste bitter on the back of my tongue. Come hell or high water, I'm going to help build her back up.

With my thoughts consumed by Fallon, I only managed to sleep a couple of hours. I'm up early and walk to my closet. My eyes scan over the different shades of gray.

Shit.

For a moment, I hesitate, thinking I should call Noah to help me, but then I take the first shirt and pants my hand touches and hope the colors will match.

There's a soft tap against my door, and I call out, "Come in."

"I made you some coffee," Fallon says as she steps inside.

I let out a thankful breath. "You're just in time. Can you help me pick a shirt and pants that match?"

"Sure." She first sets the cup down, then comes to stand next to me. "Ooh, no." She takes the items from my hands and hangs them back in the closet. "We should actually get rid of that shirt. I don't like pink on you."

I let out a burst of laughter. "You can throw it out."

"I can arrange your clothes from dark to light colors, so it's easier for you in the future," Fallon offers.

"I'd appreciate that." Seeing her take control of everything makes hope explode in my heart.

Fallon removes a shirt and pants, then holds them up against my body. "Yeah, this will do."

"T-shirt or button-up?" I ask, so I'll know whether I can actually put on the shirt without any help.

"It's cold out. There's no way I'm letting you wear a t-shirt. Put it on, then I can help with the buttons."

Hmm… I like where this is going," I tease her, then I add, "I first need to shower."

"Ah…"

I let out a burst of laughter and decide to take it easy on her. "Just set the clothes on the bed. I'll come find you when I need help with the buttons."

"I'm going to get dressed then. I'll be back in a couple of minutes."

Before she can leave, I say, "Thank you for wanting to help me."

There's a pause, then Fallon murmurs, "Thank you for letting me."

It takes me a couple of minutes longer to get through my morning routine. I've even managed to brush my teeth without any help, although I got toothpaste on my left hand.

After stepping into my pants, I shrug on the long sleeve button up, then walk to Fallon's room. As I knock on her door, Jade comes out of her and Hunter's room, and she teases, "Loving the new look. Do you need help?"

"I'm good, thanks," I say quickly. Just then, Fallon opens her door.

"Oh, wow," she whispers as her eyes lock on my chest and abs. "Ah… let's go to your room."

I follow Fallon back to my room, and shutting the door behind me, I go to stand in front of Fallon and grin down at her.

Lifting her hands to my shoulders, she first adjusts the shirt before she begins to do the buttons. Feeling her fingers brush against my chest makes anticipation grow inside me. Every inch she moves down increases the electric current that's forming between us.

Thank God the attraction is still there.

215

By the time she reaches the last button over my abs, I have to fist my hands at my sides, so I don't grab hold of her.

"Anything else you need help with?" Fallon asks, her voice low and husky.

Hearing how affected she is by me sends my blood rushing through my veins.

It takes a lot of effort to stay in control and to not give in to my need for Fallon. "Socks," I murmur. "And shoes."

"Oh, right," Fallon breathes, and then she walks back to my closet. I go sit on my unmade bed while I wait for her.

When Fallon rushes back, and she kneels in front of me, I say, "I can do this myself."

"I don't mind." She slips my socks onto my feet, then helps me stand so I can step into my shoes. "Let me just grab a sweater for you."

I haven't been dressed by a woman since I was a kid, but knowing my girl is a control freak, I let her have her way.

She comes back and pulls the sweater over my head, then arranges my collar. Brushing her hands over my shoulders, she says, "All done."

I lift my hand to her left cheek, and leaning down, I press a kiss to her forehead. "Thank you."

"Uh-huh."

"So, we have a date later?" I ask.

"What?" she gasps.

"Arranging my clothes by color," I remind her.

"Oh, sure." I can swear I hear a sliver of disappointment in her voice. I'm still thinking about ordering us food so we can have a picnic on my bedroom floor while working, but before I can mention it, Fallon darts to the door. "Have a good day. See you later."

For a minute there, I thought things were better between us, but it's clear Fallon's still awkward around me.

What did you expect? One day of being nice to her isn't going to make weeks of heartache disappear.

Patience, Kao.

Chapter 17

FALLON

Things are weird. I hardly slept, replaying the kiss and Kao telling me he loves me over and over. It feels surreal like I've slipped into a dream to avoid my devastating reality.

And then this morning. Seeing Kao's abs in all their hard and hot as hell glory made me feel overly aware of him. Helping him button his shirt was a new experience. Yeah, needless to say, it was super hard focusing on the job and not giving in to my desire to run my palms all over his chest.

A soft smile plays around my lips as Kao runs circles in my mind.

I feel frazzled... and awkward. It's like our friendship from before the accident is a distant memory. We used to be comfortable around each other, and yeah, there was attraction, but nothing compared to what I felt while helping Kao get dressed.

Maybe it's because I almost lost him?

My smile fades as a new worry begins to worm itself into my heart. I want to be with Kao… so desperately, but the scars.

My heart is torn in two. If Kao was scarred in the accident, I wouldn't care at all. I'd still love and want him.

But it's hard to think Kao would feel that way about me.

Ugh, it's such a struggle.

"Are you ready?" Mila asks, drawing me out of my thoughts.

"Yeah." I pause when I see Noah rush into Kao's room. "Give me a second." I walk down the hallway, and when I push the door open and step inside, I see Noah give Kao medication. "Is everything okay?"

Noah glances at me. "Yeah, it's just a migraine."

Concerned for Kao, I move closer. "Is there anything I can do? A cool cloth?"

"Sure," Noah answers.

My gaze flits worriedly over Kao, where he's sitting with his head resting in his hands. I go to his bathroom and rinse the washcloth under the cold water.

Rushing back to Kao, I say, "Lie back."

Gingerly he moves, and once he's lying down, I place the cloth over his forehead. I remove his shoes, and then I take a seat next to him on the bed. "Can I try something?"

"Sure," he whispers, an intense look of pain tightening his features.

Leaning over Kao, I press my fingers to his temples and rub slow circles over his skin.

A minute or so later, Kao murmurs, "That's helping."

I glance up at Noah, "Can you get me a bowl with some ice in it?"

Noah nods and heads out of the room.

"On a scale of one to ten, how bad is it?" I ask.

"It was nine, but now it's seven."

"Good," I whisper. "Hopefully, it keeps getting better."

When Noah comes back, I ask, "Can you add some water?"

Noah gets some from the bathroom, and when he sets the bowl down, I remove the cloth and soak it in the icy water.

"Stay and rest," Noah says, "I'll go through the work with you later."

"Thanks," Kao says, his voice sounding strained.

Mila peeks into the room. "Is everything okay?"

"Yeah, Kao has a migraine. I'm going to stay with him. Will you take notes for me?"

"Of course." Her worried gaze darts to Kao. "I hope you feel better soon."

Once they've left, I say, "Can you stand up? I want to get you into comfortable clothes. Maybe if you sleep a little, you'll feel better."

Kao climbs off the bed, and I work quickly to get his sweater off. I rush through the buttons and pull the shirt off, then I run to his closet. I grab a t-shirt and sweatpants. Hurrying back to him, I hardly take in his body as I help him out of his pants. Once I have him in the comfy clothes, I say, "Lie back down." I press the water out of the cloth, then gently brush it over his forehead. "Tell me if it's too cold."

"It feels really good," he murmurs. The corner of his mouth lifts slightly. "Never thought the first time you undress me would be like this."

A burst of laughter escapes me and wanting him to feel better, I tease, "I hardly got to take in anything. I feel cheated. We'll have to do a repeat once you're better."

Kao chuckles but instantly stops, and a flash of pain tightens his features again. I rinse the cloth and let it rest over his forehead so I can massage his temples.

221

After a couple of minutes, Kao says, "I haven't had the eyedrops yet. Will you be able to help me?"

"Of course." I glance at the three bottles next to his bed. "Is there a specific order?"

"No."

Reaching for the first bottle, I uncap it then lean over Kao. Feeling nervous, I whisper, "Tell me if I do something wrong."

I drop the liquid into his eyes and watch as he blinks. Sitting back, I put the bottle down on its place, then I ask, "For how long do you have to use the eye drops?"

"The doctor didn't say. It all depends on the healing, but it will probably be for a year or more."

"I'll have to get used to this then," I tease, and it makes the corner of Kao's mouth lift again.

I administer the other two bottles, waiting a couple of minutes in between like Noah told me. When I'm done, I ask, "How do you feel?"

"If I say bad will you stay?" Kao asks, making me grin at him.

"I'm already late for class, so I have nowhere to be." I glance at his closet. "I might as well arrange your clothes now."

"That sounds like a good idea," Kao chuckles. "Then I can take you for dinner later."

I instantly freeze, feeling a tremor of shock.

My silence has Kao saying, "If it's too soon, we can wait?"

I shake my head, then stammer, "Are… are you asking me on a date?"

"Yes, and seeing as the first attempt was such an epic fuck up, I have some serious damage control to do."

I still feel the embers of heartbreak, but my hope of being with Kao keeps growing by the second, and it makes me feel over-emotional.

We were so happy together.

Now Kao's fighting to get his sight back, and I have hideous scars.

"Fallon?" Kao whispers. His eyes soften on me, and he reaches a hand up, taking hold of my arm. "Are you okay?"

I shake my head. "It's so unfair," I whisper. "I can't… believe what happened to us."

"We'll be okay," he murmurs, and sitting up, he pulls me into his arms.

I've heard those words from everyone and never believed them for a second. But hearing Kao say them is really all I needed.

KAO

Not wanting to let go of Fallon, I say, "We didn't get much sleep last night. Wanna nap with me?"

She nods, and I quickly move to the middle of the bed.

"Just taking off my shoes."

When she's done, she first drops the cloth back in the water, and it has me saying, "You can leave it off. The migraine is starting to fade."

"Good." Fallon slides into bed next to me, and I hold my right arm open so she can lie down against me. When her body curls into mine, I bring my left hand to her head and press her down on my shoulder.

She stiffens for a moment, and knowing why, I murmur, "Don't worry about the scars. They don't bother me at all."

After a couple of seconds, Fallon whispers, "I can't help but think of them. They're hideous."

Turning on my side so I can face her, I hold her tightly to my chest. "You're still the most beautiful woman to me."

Fallon presses closer to me, hiding her face against my chest.

Feeling she needs to understand how important she is to me, I admit, "I never got to tell you, and if it's one thing this whole ordeal taught me, it's that tomorrow is not guaranteed." I pull a little back, and as my eyes try to focus on her face, I wish my sight would return this moment so I can see every detail of her and the color of her eyes. Pushing my own struggle to the side, I continue, "You are the most important person in my life, Fallon. You're my beginning and end. That's why I lost my shit when I heard you got hurt. If anything were to happen to you because of me, I wouldn't survive."

"But it wasn't your fault. The truck driver fell asleep and crashed into us," Fallon reminds me.

"Still, it's my duty to protect you, and I feel like I failed you."

"You didn't," she whispers, emotion welling in her voice.

We're moving off-topic now, and I need to bring my point across. "No matter what you look like or what happens in the future, I love you, and I always will. I'll never let you down again. I promise."

I hear her breath hitch, and then she asks, "Do you pity —"

Before she can finish the sentence, the words burst from me, "No!" I bring my hand to her chin and nudge her face up until I feel her breaths fluttering over my jaw. "I absolutely hate that you got hurt." I shake my head. "I respect you too much to pity you, Fallon."

Her fingers wrap around my wrist. "Thank you, Kao. I needed to hear that."

Having Fallon in my bed and feeling her breath on my face makes anticipation begin to build in me.

More than anything, I want to kiss her right now. Yesterday it happened suddenly, and it was so emotionally charged, I didn't get to savor her.

I inch a little closer and whisper, "Can I kiss you?"

A tense moment passes before she nods. "Yes."

Getting her permission, I focus on her breaths warming my face, until there's nothing but Fallon. Slowly, leaning in, my lips brush against hers. I pull back and breathe in her exhales as they speed up. My eyes drift shut as I press my mouth to hers. Using my body, I push against Fallon until she's flat on her back. I tilt my head and breathing in her intoxicating scent, my lips begin to move.

Fuck, it's hard to keep the kiss slow.

My tongue brushes against her bottom lip, begging for entrance, and the moment she opens for me and I get to taste her, my self-control slips. The kiss becomes more intense, our tongues exploring each other. A soft moan drifts from Fallon, robbing me of all my senses and the urge to consume her overwhelms me.

My teeth scrape over her bottom lip before my tongue plunges back into the warmth of her mouth. It feels like our lips are melting together, and I can't get enough of how good she tastes.

I always knew kissing Fallon would change my world, but I never knew how much. She's become my every breath, and I know I won't survive a minute without her.

Even if my sight never fully returns, I won't be able to let go of her.

My hand slips over her cheek and into her hair, and wanting to show her that I love every inch of her, even the scars, I break the kiss and feather kisses over her cheek.

Chapter 18

FALLON

When Kao's lips brush over the scars, it takes every bit of strength I have not to pull away. A war erupts in me, half of me wanting to hide my disfigurement from him, and the other half needing to feel that he accepts me as I am.

Kao's mouth comes back to mine, and he presses a soft kiss to my lips before pulling back. "I'll never be able to let you go again."

His words make tears push up my throat, but I swallow them back down and whisper, "Promise?"

"I promise."

Kao pulls me against his chest, and I feel his breath on my forehead, then he lets out a chuckle. "God, now that I've kissed you, it's all I want to do."

"You took your sweet time," I playfully chastise him. "I know you said we should take things slowly, but I never thought you meant *this* slow."

My teasing draws another chuckle from him. "I'm done taking things slow." He pauses for a moment, then asks, "Can I take you to dinner tonight? It won't be any place spectacular, just the campus restaurant."

Grinning, I nod as I wrap my arm around his waist. "I'd love that."

We lie in silence for a while, then I ask, "How's the migraine?"

A mischievous smile spreads over his face. "Instantly cured, the second your lips touched mine."

We grow quiet, and I try to process everything that's happened between us. From the heartache to the kiss, my life feels like a coin being flipped in the air, and God only knows where it will land.

Lying in Kao's arms, and feeling the warmth from his body, makes me swallow hard on the emotions whirling in me.

I really thought I lost him. It's scary how convincing he was.

"What are you thinking?" Kao whispers, his arms tightening around me.

Hesitant to bring it up again, I say, "Nothing."

Kao pulls back a little. "I can feel you thinking."

"It's just..." still feeling apprehensive, I have to force the words out, "you were really convincing when you told me you only wanted to be friends."

Kao brings his hand to my right cheek, and I instantly cringe, but he doesn't let it stop him from tenderly brushing my hair back and tucking the strands behind my ear. "I just wanted to protect you. In hindsight, I was stupid as fuck."

"You got so angry with me," I murmur, my brows drawing together as the residual heartache clenches my heart. "I've never seen you behave that way, and it was scary," I admit.

Kao presses a kiss to my lips, then says, "I'm sorry."

I lift my eyes to his, and my throat closes as I say, "Please don't hurt me again."

"Never." His eyes caress my face, and there's only love shining from them. "I promise."

"It's so frightening how much power you have," I admit my biggest fear to him. "You control my happiness."

Kao kisses me again. "I'll protect you every day of my life, even from myself."

KAO

Having Fallon be so honest with me about her feelings only makes me feel more protective of her. Control is everything to her. Knowing she's laying her future happiness in my hands is a task I take seriously.

I brush my fingers over her hair and press another quick kiss to her mouth. Pulling an inch apart, it feels like we're caught in our own little world.

My hand moves to her cheek, and my fingertips carefully caress her scars. I can feel the raised skin unevenly stretching all the way from her cheek down to her collar bone.

When she squirms under my touch, I whisper, "I love you, Fallon."

I hear her breath hitch, and then she buries her face under my chin. Her voice sounds fragile as she says, "It looks like my face and neck shattered." A soft sob bursts over my chest, and I wrap her tightly against me. "It's red and... all angry."

I push Fallon onto her back and pull her face away from my chest. Using my thumbs, I brush the tears I feel on her cheeks away. "You're still the most beautiful woman I've ever seen." Leaning down, I caress every scar with my lips.

I know I'll have to keep reminding her they don't matter to me, and I'll do it a million times a day if that's what she needs.

"I…" she hesitates before she admits, "I don't feel like a woman anymore."

Christ.

"Fallon," I breathe, shocked by how acutely the scars are affecting her. I position my body over hers, and the moment my pelvis presses against the gap between her legs, my cock reacts. I rest my forearms on either side of her head and press a tender kiss to her quivering lips. "Can you feel me?"

"Yeah," she whispers.

"Trust me when I say, you're a breathtakingly beautiful woman." I press my cock harder against her, and I feel a burst of pleasure. "It's only because I know you need time that I'm not ripping your clothes off right now."

She hesitates, but sucking in a deep breath, she asks, "Do you really want me like that?"

"Are you asking whether I want to make love to you?" I ask to clarify, my eyes locked on hers. I rub my cock against her and lean closer until our breaths mix. "Cause the answer is an absolute, I'm aching to be inside you, yes."

It's becoming increasingly difficult not to give in to my desire for her. I want our first time together to be special, but God, my hands are itching to explore her.

Fallon lifts her head, and her mouth crashes against mine. Her kiss grows with urgency, and I let her have all the control, knowing how much it means to her.

Unable to keep still, I slip my left hand down to her hip and begin to slowly thrust against her.

Fuck, I'm going to explode in my sweatpants if we keep going down this path.

I tilt my head as our tongues hungrily stroke against each other. With almost zero self-control left, my hand slips under her cashmere sweater, and I caress the stretch of skin beneath her ribs.

She's silky smooth, and I can feel her body heat increasing as our mouths devour each other.

My cock thrusts hard against her, and the pleasure is so intense it makes lights burst behind my eyelids. Breaking the kiss, I gasp for air. "God, Fallon. You're making me see lights."

"What? Really?" she asks, excitement coloring her voice.

I nod, a wide smile spreading over my face. "If we don't stop now, I'm going to lose control," I warn her, not wanting to push her too fast.

Fallon lifts her hand to my cheek, and her touch is tender. I can picture her eyes turning to liquid gold as she says, "I need you, Kao. Haven't we waited long enough?"

Hearing her say those words to me restores some of my manhood I've lost due to my independence being almost non-existent. I don't feel totally useless anymore. Loving Fallon gives me a purpose, and if that's all I'll ever be good for, I'll die a happy man.

But then I start to think of the technical part of sex. "We have a small problem, though."

Fallon's voice is cautious as she asks, "What?"

I let out an embarrassed chuckle. "The condom. You'll have to help me put it on. That's the last thing we want to screw up."

This is not the conversation I wanted to have with her right before we make love for the first time.

"Also, what's the time? We don't want Noah walking in on us," I voice another worry.

The moment fades, and wanting our first time together being more special than this, I say, "Maybe we should continue making out? When I make love to you, I don't want it to be here in the suite."

A wide smile stretches over Fallon's face as she teases me, "You just had an entire conversation with yourself." She presses a soft kiss to my mouth. "It's cute when you overthink things." Another kiss. "I'm good with making out."

When our mouths touch again, I don't let her pull back, and I nip at her bottom lip. "It's so hot when you do that," Fallon murmurs against my mouth.

"This?" I ask, my voice low in my throat, and then I bite her bottom lip before thrusting my tongue into her mouth and kissing her hungrily.

Shifting my body half off of her and pushing her sweater up, my hand caresses her skin until I reach her breast. My thumb skims over her puckered nipple, and it draws a groan from me.

Pulling her bra out of the way, I cover her breast. Kneading her, my touch grows harder and my kiss more desperate, and I begin to forget all the reasons why we shouldn't have sex right now.

A knock on my door has me pulling back so fast, I almost fall off the side of the bed, but Fallon grabs hold of me as a burst of laughter bubbles over her lips.

Climbing over her, I lie down beside her and throw my arm over my face as I chuckle. I manage to ask, "Are you decent?"

"Almost." A couple of seconds later, she calls out, "Come in?"

The door opens, and I hear Noah ask, "Fallon, did you give him his eye drops?"

"Yeah, a while back," she answers.

"How's the migraine?"

"Gone," I reply while sitting up, "We should probably get some breakfast."

"You mean lunch," Noah teases. "It's already twelve."

"Shit? Seriously?" Fallon gasps, and I feel as she begins to scoot off the bed.

Reaching for her, I grab hold of her arm and yank her back against me. "I'm holding you hostage for the day."

"That's my queue to leave," Noah mutters. "Remember the eye drops at two."

Noah shuts the door behind him. I push Fallon down and straddle her hips. My hands brush up her body until I reach her arms, and I pin them down to the bed. Then I lean down, and keeping my voice low, I say, "We have a month to make up for. Skip classes today and stay with me."

Without thinking about it, she answers, "Okay."

Grinning, I playfully say, "We can play nurse and patient."

Laughter dances in her voice as she asks, "Should I check your temperature?"

Leaning down, I ask, "And how would you do that?"

Fallon lifts her head and murmurs, "With my mouth." She presses a quick kiss to my lips. "Nah, no fever."

Chuckling, I say, "Give it time. I can feel my temperature rising."

Fallon pulls her arms free and places her hands on my thighs.

"Yep, especially with your hands so close to my cock," I tease her.

Laughing, she begins to squirm out from under me. "Come on, we should get food."

Pretending to sulk, I climb off the bed, then I grin, "Does this mean you're dressing me again?"

"No, we're ordering in."

When she begins to walk toward the door, I say, "I need a minute before I can go out there."

"Why?" Fallon instantly darts back to me.

Wrapping an arm around her waist, I pull her tightly against me. "I'm still hard for you."

"Oh," she says, a little breathlessly.

I let go of her. "Order anything you want. I'll be out in a couple of minutes."

"Okay." When Fallon leaves, I sit back down on the edge of the bed.

It feels like we've taken a considerable leap in the right direction. This morning has easily been the best in my entire life.

Chapter 19

FALLON

While I was alone with Kao in his room, I began to forget about the scars. But the moment I walk down the hallway, the insecurities rush back, and I quickly dart into my room to brush my hair so it will cover the right side of my face.

Sitting down on the stool by my dressing table, I pull the bristles through my hair. My movements still, and I stare at my reflection.

Being with Kao, I felt like the old me and not this scarred woman. Feeling his desire for me, his kisses and touches – they all made the world fade away.

Slowly, I lift my hand, and I pull the hair away from my cheek. Revulsion builds in my chest as my eyes lock on the swollen red gashes. There's a thick jagged one, stretching from my ear down my neck.

I let my hair fall back and take a deep breath.

I can't help but wonder if Kao is pretending the scars don't bother him for my sake.

You wouldn't care if Kao was disfigured.

I love him so much, and I want to be with him more than anything, but my trust has taken a blow. I guess only time will tell whether he'll stay with me.

The thought makes my apprehension grow, and my shoulders slump.

I wish none of this had happened.

"Fallon?" I hear Kao call, and then he walks into my room. "Are you okay?"

"Oh, yeah," I answer, injecting happiness into my voice. "Just brushed my hair. It was all over the place." I get up and walk to him. "Let's order food."

We go sit in the living room, and I place an order with the restaurant, then I ask, "What do you want to do while we wait?"

He lifts an arm around my shoulder and pulls me into his side. "I want to ask you a favor."

"Yeah?" I glance up at him.

"I have a follow-up appointment with my ophthalmologist on Thursday. Will you go with me?"

I don't hesitate to answer, "Of course."

"Will you be okay driving us there?"

"Yes." I pause for a moment then ask, "Will you be okay with me driving?"

Kao nods. "We have to get back together in a car at some point. The sooner, the better." The corner of his mouth lifts. "Besides, I trust you."

My lips curve up, and I snuggle into his side. "What time is your appointment?"

"At ten."

"I'll ask Mila to take notes for me," I say, making a mental note to remember.

"I'm already keeping you out of class today. Will you be okay missing another day? I can always ask my dad."

"No, I want to go with you," I rush to answer.

There's a knock at the front door, and I get up to answer. Collecting our food, I carry it to the counter. "Food's here."

While Kao comes to sit at the table, I plate our food and get two bottles of water from the fridge. I place Kao's plate and water in front of him and say, "I got us roasted vegetables and steak. I wasn't sure, so I cut your steak into pieces."

A nervous grin spreads over Kao's face. "Thank you."

I sit down next to him and watch as he tries to spear a piece of meat. Watching him struggle, my heart shrinks into a painful lump. Unable to sit still, I reach for his hand and stop him. "Can I help?"

Kao pauses and shifts on the stool, a frown forming on his forehead.

"Don't be embarrassed, Kao," I murmur as I scoot my stool closer to him. "Let me feed my man."

My comment makes the corner of his mouth lift slightly. "This is foreplay for you, isn't it?"

I let out a chuckle as I spear a square of steak. "Yeah, it's a total turn-on." I bring the food to his mouth and say, "Open wide."

Kao lets out an awkward breath, but he takes the bite. After chewing and swallowing, he mutters, "Not my greatest moment."

I lean closer and let my breath skim over his ear, then I whisper, "I already felt you hard between my legs. Nothing will make me see you as less of a man."

Kao's hand comes up, and he wraps his fingers around the back of my neck. "Now I want to drag you back to my room and finish what we started."

"Be a good boyfriend and eat all your food, and I might just let you," I tease him.

"Are you resorting to bribing me now?" He asks a playful expression dancing on his face.

I spear a carrot. "Yup. Open up."

Movement catches my eye, and I glance to the hallway. Jase is watching us with a soft smile on his face. When our eyes meet, it widens into a grin. Then he turns and heads back to his room.

KAO

I'm not going to lie, lunch was hard. Having Fallon feed me chipped away at my self-esteem. I didn't have the heart to tell her it was because she cut the steak into tiny pieces. Mostly I can make out food, just nothing small. Everything blurs together then.

Fuck, my eyes need to come right.

Fallon wanted to take a nap, and long after she's fallen asleep, I feel way too restless to keep lying in bed. I move slowly, so I won't wake her and quietly leave my room.

When I walk into the living room, I see Hana, where she's sitting on the couch.

I take a seat on the other couch. "Hey, can I ask you a favor?"

"Sure, what's up?"

"I want to do something special for Fallon tonight. Can you help me arrange everything?"

"Of course." Hana gets up and comes to drop down next to me. "What do you need me to do?"

I tell her what I have in mind, and she helps me make all the calls.

When all the arrangements are made, I say, "Thanks, I couldn't have done it without you."

"You're welcome." Hana turns her body to face me and asks, "How are you doing?"

"I'm getting there. I just wish my eyes would heal quicker."

She leans closer to me. "At least the color of your eyes didn't change. Oh wow, the stitches look cool."

"They only did a cornea transplant," I tease her, then I explain. "It's basically the gel layer over the iris."

"What can you see?"

"I can see your face and what you're wearing." I focus on Hana's face, then add, "Just not the finer details and no color. My sight's still very blurry."

She places her hand on mine. "I'm sure it will keep getting better." Then Hana pulls back and says, "I wanted to talk to you about something."

"Yeah?"

"The way you treated Fallon," Hana begins, and instantly my stomach drops.

I square my shoulders, ready for a tongue lashing, which I totally deserve.

Hana takes a deep breath, then asks, "Why did you hurt her like that?"

"First, I blamed myself for her getting hurt, and then I didn't want to saddle her with a blind man," I explain.

"Have you worked through those feelings?" she asks.

"Yeah, and I explained everything to Fallon."

"Kao," I can hear the warning coming, "if you ever hurt my friend like that again, Jase will be the last person you should watch out for. I love Fallon more than anything, and seeing her broken like that..." Hana pauses, her voice quivering with emotion, "You didn't just break her heart."

Fuck, I feel like shit.

Lifting an arm, I wrap it around Hana's shoulder and pull her into a hug. "I'm sorry, Hana."

"Just be the man she deserves," she murmurs as she hugs me back.

"I will."

When we pull away from each other, Hana says, "I have to admit, tonight's date is a good start."

Letting out a chuckle, I say, "I hope she likes it."

245

Hana gives my arm a squeeze, and then she gets up. "She will. I'll go wake her so she can start getting ready."

"Thank you."

When Hana disappears down the hallway, and I stare at the coffee table. After a while, my sight sharpens, and I see clearer.

I let out a breath, and the corner of my mouth curves up.

It's only a matter of time before I'll be able to see fine details and color.

Chapter 20

FALLON

"How about this dress?" Hana asks as she holds it up.

"It's only dinner at the campus restaurant," I argue. "Jeans and a sweater will be fine."

"Like hell," Hana growls. "You're wearing a dress." She disappears back into my closet and comes out with a pair of heels. "And these babies."

"Hana, it's cold out," I complain.

"That's why they invented coats. Stop arguing and put on some lipstick."

We've been at this for hours, but I can't help smile at her determination to get me all dressed up.

"What's Kao wearing?" I ask before I swipe on some lipgloss.

"I'll go check quickly." She darts out of the room.

Getting up from the stool, I walk over to my bed, and I look down at the form-fitting white and silver gown I got from *Donna Karan* for the Christmas Ball. There's a sad twinge in my chest, but knowing Hana won't back down, I go to my closet and pick a black scarf to match the shoes, then I get dressed.

Hana comes back into my room as I carefully wrap the scarf around my neck to keep my hair in place.

She scrunches her nose at me. "I wish you wouldn't do that. It will be dark outside soon, and no one will be able to see."

I shake my head. "I'm not taking any chances. The scars are the last thing I want to worry about tonight."

She pulls a disgruntled face but then smiles. "You look gorgeous." She gestures toward my door. "Your prince awaits."

I let out a chuckle as I pick up my clutch.

"Wait, the coat," Hana gasps. She darts into my closet, and a couple of seconds later, she comes back with my black coat.

Taking it from her, I drape it over my arm and say, "Thanks for all the help. It was actually fun."

"Have an amazing night."

I walk out of my room, and when I enter the shared living space, Noah's eyes widen on me. "Holy shit, you look stunning."

"Thanks, Noah."

248

My gaze locks on Kao, and the breath rushes from my lungs. He's dressed to the nines in a dark charcoal suit.

God, he's breathtaking.

He stares at me, his lips parted, and wonder settles on his face. The way Kao looks at me makes me feel beautiful, and a little of my crushed self-esteem trickles back.

I walk closer to him. "You look impressive, Mr. Reed."

The corner of his mouth lifts. "You're a vision to behold, Miss Reyes."

I let out a chuckle. "Are you ready?"

Kao holds his hand out to me, and I take another step closer to him. Lifting my hand, I place it in his, and instantly tingles spread up my arm.

This man is so intense, even his touch is electric.

"Enjoy the night, kids," Hana calls after us as we walk out of the suite.

When we stop in front of the elevator, Kao murmurs, "God, you smell good."

The doors open, and we step inside. Kao's fingers tighten around mine, and then he says, "We're not going to the restaurant."

"Oh?" A smile tugs at my lips. "Where are we going?"

Kao lets out a chuckle, "You'll have to wait and see."

As we walk out of our building, Summer comes rushing around the corner, but then she pauses. "Wow, you both look beautiful. Enjoy the evening."

I watch her dart away before I can even reply.

Did Kao...? Nah... But...

I look up at him. "Are we going to the hall?"

"Damn, I knew you'd catch on," he says, a broad smile stretching over his face. "I figured since we missed the Christmas Ball and you worked really hard on it, you should at least experience it."

My heart. Can he be any more thoughtful?

A happy smile begins to play around my lips as I cautiously lead Kao to the hall. When we step inside, and I see all the decorations, my smile turns into a bubble of laughter. "It looks so good. I love the winter wonderland theme," I murmur.

There's only one table situated in the middle of the hall, and a band is ready in the corner.

"Are we going to dance?" I ask, a fluttering of anticipation in my chest.

"Of course," Kao states.

Kao pulls my chair out for me. "Thank you," I murmur as I sit down. Kao presses a kiss to the top of my head.

The waiter brings a sprite for Kao and a coke for me, then he hurries out of the hall.

"I hope you don't mind, but I already placed an order with the kitchen," Kao says. "I'm having pizza, so you don't have to feed me."

"Shoot, there you go and spoil all the fun," I tease him.

He chuckles, then asks, "Are you okay with the seafood platter? I know you love it and felt it was a safe bet."

I reach over the table for his hand and give it a squeeze. "That sounds perfect. Kinda like my man taking charge. I could get used to this."

"Your man?" His mouth lifts into the sexy grin I love so much.

"Yeah," I murmur.

"So, you're good with us being in a relationship?" Kao asks.

"Yeah, so much for taking our time, right?" I laugh. "I should've known you'd just sweep me right off my feet again."

"I won't let you fall this time."

Kao's words make emotion well in my chest. I stare at him, feeling so thankful that we found our way back to each other.

"I love you, Kao."

KAO

Finally, hearing those words from Fallon, my life feels complete, and I realize there would be nothing worse than living a life without her.

I rub my thumb over the back of her hand and say, "You've just made me the happiest man alive."

Fuck, she looks absolutely breathtaking in the dress. I just hate that she's covering half her face and wish I could reach over and tuck the hair behind her ear. Not wanting to ruin the night, I keep still.

A server brings our food, and once he steps away from the table, Fallon says, "All dressed up, and things are about to get messy," Fallon jokes. "This is perfect."

While we eat, the band plays background music. The atmosphere is peaceful, and I'm grateful the night is going according to plan.

"Earlier, I was sitting in the living room, and for a moment, the blurriness faded a little," I tell Fallon.

"Oh, my God! That's great," Fallon exclaims. "Give or take two to three weeks, and you should start seeing color, right?"

"Yeah, it's hard to predict. Every person heals differently. With a little luck, I'll be back to normal by the end of the month."

"Yeah, we'll have plenty to celebrate then."

I take a bite, and after swallowing, I say, "You should join the decorating committee again."

Fallon pauses for a moment. "We'll see after the surgery."

"I'll go with you to the meetings," I try to encourage her. "Hell, you can even give me work to do."

"Why do you want me to join it again?"

"You loved it, Fallon," I explain. "I want you doing the things that bring you happiness."

"You know what would make me happy?" she asks.

"What?"

"Us dancing." I hear the playful tone in her voice, and not wanting to upset her, I drop the subject of the decorating committee.

Standing up, I hold my hand out to her. Fallon moves around the table, and taking hold of my hand, we walk to the dance floor.

The band instantly stops the song they're playing, and a moment later, the guy sings the opening notes to *Stand By Me* by *John Newman*.

Placing one hand on her side, I take a step closer to her. We begin to dance to the song I picked specifically for this moment. It says everything I feel.

"Kao," Fallon whispers, her voice quivering with emotion. She moves her arms around my neck and holds me tightly as the words drift to us.

I wrap her in a tight embrace and press a kiss to the side of her head. "Thank you for standing by me."

She nods against my chest, and I feel her body jerk.

"Turned out I wasn't so perfect," I try to joke, but the moment is too emotionally charged.

Fallon pulls back, and then she presses her mouth to mine. Tasting her tears, I bring my hands to her face, and using my thumbs, I brush them away.

She pulls back and whispers, "You are perfect."

"Only in your eyes," I tease. A sense of Deja vu washes over me, sending goosebumps racing over my skin. "Damn, that felt weird, like we've done this before."

"We did," Fallon says. "Right before we were hit by the truck."

Not wanting the night to take a turn for the worse, I say, "Guess that means we're really meant to be."

"How do you figure that?" she asks, laughter in her voice.

"We didn't get it right the first time, so fate intervened and gave us a repeat."

"Like a do-over?" she asks.

"Yeah."

Just then, the band begins to play *Never Enough* by *Lauren Allred*. Their timing couldn't be more perfect.

Fallon and I move slowly over the floor as the music weaves a spell around us. As the tempo builds, I feel the moment deep in my bones, and it's incredible.

As the singer utters the last words, I lean down and press a kiss to Fallon's lips. She leans into my arm as we walk back to the table, and once we've taken our seats, she says, "Thank you for an amazing first date."

Chapter 21

FALLON

Even though things between Kao and me are better than they've ever been, I'm anxious about taking him for his follow up appointment today.

It will be our first time together in a car since the accident, and I pray nothing goes wrong.

Taking a deep breath, I walk to the living room and find Kao waiting. He's sitting on a couch, and I notice his right knee jumping.

He's nervous as well.

I push my own anxiety down and say, "Let's go. I'd rather be early than late."

Kao gets up, and I hold my hand out to him. When our fingers interweave, I give him a squeeze. "I'll drive slow."

"I trust you," he replies, and hearing the sincerity, I frown.

"You seem nervous?"

"I'm just anxious about what the doctor will say." He gives me an encouraging grin. "Hopefully, it's all good news."

"I'm sure it will go well."

We walk out of the suite, and by the time we reach my car, my stomach is tight with knots.

Kao stops me before I can open the driver's side door, and he wraps me in a hug, pressing a kiss to my mouth. "We're going to be fine. Okay? You've got this."

I let out an anxious breath and then climb into the car.

When we both have our seat belts on, I suck in a deep breath of air and start the engine.

Please let nothing bad happen.

My heart begins to pound as I steer the vehicle out of the campus gates. It feels like I'm learning to drive all over again, my eyes darting everywhere. I grip the steering wheel hard, painfully ready should another car swerve in our direction.

Suddenly Kao says, "Will you go away with me this coming weekend?"

I quickly wet my dry lips, then asks, "Where?"

"Where it will be just the two of us. Rancho Valencia in Rancho Santa Fe?"

"That's a three-hour drive," I squeak, far from ready to spend that long in a car.

"I'll arrange a helicopter."

My mouth curves up. "You've thought about everything, haven't you?"

"Of course," he chuckles. "I've booked a villa from tomorrow night through to Sunday afternoon."

"What if I said no," I tease him.

"I was willing to risk it."

"What time are we leaving tomorrow?" I ask as I pull the car into the parking area outside the medical center.

"Five o'clock?"

"Sounds good," I grin as I turn off the engine, and then I let out a relieved breath. "We made it."

"I never doubted you for a second," Kao murmurs as we climb out of the car.

When we walk into the doctor's office, Kao stops by the reception. "Kao Reed. I have an appointment at ten."

"Take a seat. Dr. Hodgson will be with you in a minute," the receptionist says with a sweet smile.

The instant we sit down, I rest my hand on Kao's thigh. I know I'm being possessive, but the receptionist looked a little too friendly in my opinion.

Kao covers my hand with his own, and he leans into me so he can whisper, "I can't wait to get this behind me so we can go back to the suite and make out."

I smile at him, and turning my hand over beneath his, I weave our fingers together. "My hermit. We'll have to live in the mountains once we're married."

"You'd do that for me?" he grins happily.

"Of course. I know how much you hate being around people."

"Except you," he murmurs lovingly.

"The doctor will see you now," the receptionist calls, popping our happy bubble.

"Should I wait?" I ask Kao, but he shakes his head and pulls me to my feet.

I stick close to his side as we walk down a short hallway and then into an office.

"Good to see you, Mr. Reed," Dr. Hodgson says, and they shake hands.

"You too." Kao gestures to me, and then he chuckles. "I brought my girlfriend for support."

The doctor spares me a smile as I sit down on a chair that's situated against the opposite wall.

Dr. Hodgson gestures for Kao to sit behind some heavy eye equipment. "How do you feel?"

259

"Much better. The itchiness and pain are gone. Mostly my eyes just feel scratchy," Kao answers.

"How are the migraines?"

I have to press my lips together to not answer on behalf of Kao.

"I had a bad one yesterday. I don't get them as often anymore," Kao replies.

"Okay, how many fingers am I holding up?"

"Two."

Dr. Hodgon's moves back. "Now?"

"Four."

He steps all the way back to where I am. "And Now."

Kao pauses for a while before he murmurs, "I think four."

"That's good." Dr. Hodgson goes to take a seat opposite Kao, and he inspects his left eye first. "Look up. Down. Left. Right. Straight ahead." A couple of seconds later, Dr. Hodgson says, "Pressure check."

I clasp my hands on my lap, my gaze glued to Kao.

"The pressure looks good. Your left eye is eighteen, and the right fifteen. I'm pretty happy."

"That's good," Kao chuckles.

I have no idea what that means, but I'm happy the doctor seems pleased.

Dr. Hodgson's stares long into Kao's eyes, then he says, "The graft has attached nicely. The corneas are crystal clear. I don't see any air bubbles, which is good." He shifts closer to Kao again. "Look straight ahead for me."

Then Dr. Hodgson gets up. "If your eyes become foggy or cloudy, I want you to call us. Don't rub or push against your eyes, but so far, everything looks good."

Kao moves out from behind the equipment, a relieved expression on his face as he smiles at the doctor. "That's good to hear."

"The blurry vision will start to get better, and you'll start to see finer details soon."

"And color?" Kao asks.

"Like I mentioned before, you'll see primary colors first, probably red. Don't be surprised if you wake up one morning and you can see color. The blurriness will take longer to fade, though."

"Will I need prescription glasses?" Kao asks.

"I don't think so. Let's wait to see what your vision settles on."

They shake hands again, and just like that, the appointment comes to an end. I expected it to take much longer. When I rise to my feet, Kao comes to take hold of my hand.

"See you in a month, unless a problem pops up," Dr. Hodgson says with a pleased smile.

"Have a good day," I murmur before we leave.

KAO

I let out a breath of relief as we leave the medical center. There's always the worry that my body will reject the donor tissue. Hearing my eyes are healing well, eases my worry.

Before we reach the car, I lift Fallon's hand and press a kiss to her thumb. "Thank you for bringing me."

"I thought it would take longer," she mentions as she unlocks the doors. "I'm glad it's all good news."

After we climb in the car, I say, "I can't wait for the color to return."

During the drive back to campus, I feel Fallon growing tense again. "Are you excited for the weekend?"

"Yeah, we've never gone away." She quickly adds, "Just the two of us."

"I like the sound of that," I murmur while grinning.

A smile flutters around her mouth. "Going away with me?"

"No, just the two of us."

We make it back to Trinity in one piece, and the instant we're out of the car, I pull Fallon into a hug. "That's one milestone conquered."

"Yeah, I feel better now," Fallon admits against my chest. She lifts her face to mine, and I press a kiss to her lips. "First food, then a nap."

"Sounds amazing," I chuckle.

Once we're back in the suite, Fallon places an order with the restaurant while I grab us each a bottle of water.

"The order won't take long. I'm just going to change into sweatpants and a t-shirt," Fallon says before she disappears down the hallway.

I might as well do the same. I walk to my room and change into comfortable clothes before tidying my bed, so it's not a mess when we come to take a nap.

When I walk back into the shared space, Fallon's sitting at the island in the kitchen. My eyes glide over the hair hanging in her face, and it grates against my insides.

Moving to her, I lift my hand and brush her hair back. She quickly turns her face away. "Don't do that," I whisper as I take hold of her chin to turn her face back to me. "Let me see my beautiful girlfriend." I lean forward and press my lips to her scars. Keeping still, I take a deep breath of her, then I pull back and lock eyes with her. "God, you're breathtaking."

Her chin trembles, and she swallows hard as she drops her gaze from mine. "Only two weeks."

There's a knock at the door, but I first press a kiss to her forehead before I go to answer. I take the food from the delivery guy and carry it to the counter. "What did you get us?"

"Vegetables. Lots of veggies. You've been eating too much junk food," she chastises me.

I pull a playful disgruntled face as I open the container, and sure enough, Fallon ordered a vegetable platter. I can't even make out half of the food, but not wanting to disappoint Fallon, I keep my face expressionless.

"Humor me," Fallon chuckles. "You can have a burger for dinner."

"I can live with that," I joke.

Able to make out the corn on the cob, I pick one up. Fallon pops something that looks like a mushroom in her mouth, and before I can take another bite of the corn, she brings her fork to my mouth and whispers, "Open."

I do as she orders, and when I taste the mushroom, the corner of my mouth lifts.

When we're done with our way too healthy lunch, I grab Fallon's hand and drag her to my room. "I was a good boy, and I ate all my veggies." I grin at her as I shut the door behind us, and this time I lock it. "Now for dessert."

Fallon lets out a burst of laughter as she climbs onto my bed. "What kind of dessert?"

Placing my knee on the mattress, I crawl over her. Lowering my head, I gently bite her bottom lip, then murmur, "Your mouth." I press a kiss to her neck. "Your skin." Moving down her chest, I push up her shirt, and my teeth scrape over her hip. "All of you."

Fallon's voice is low as she teases, "What happens if someone walks in on us?"

"I locked the door," I growl as I push her sweatpants' waistband a little lower. Glancing up at her and seeing her eyes focused on me, I say, "Unless you're tired and you want to sleep."

She shakes her head, and it has me crawling back up her body until I'm braced over her. Bringing my hand to her right cheek, I brush the hair away, and keeping my palm over her scars, I press my mouth to hers. Deepening the kiss, I settle my lower body between her legs, wanting her to feel how hard I am for her.

This moment is not about finding pleasure, but to show Fallon how much I love and desire her.

Chapter 22

FALLON

Kao's kisses have a way of drugging me until I'm high on the taste of him. When his muscled body presses against mine, there are no scars – and I feel feminine beneath him.

The power Kao has over me is no longer scary, but instead, freeing and safe.

His tongue brushes hard strokes against mine, and his teeth nip at my lips, making my stomach tighten with anticipation as my desire for him grows.

When his pelvis settles against mine, and I feel how hard he is, it causes an explosion of flutters in my abdomen.

I begin to tug at his shirt, wanting it off so I can explore the hard planes of his chest and abs. Kao breaks the kiss and grabbing hold of the collar, he yanks the shirt over his head.

My eyes instantly drop, and I feast on the sight of his muscles moving as he tosses the fabric on the floor.

How's it possible that someone can look so... incredible. Even his abs line up in perfect blocks, and a sculptured V is visible from his low-hanging sweatpants.

Placing my palms on his shoulders, I brush them down over his chest, memorizing every dip and swell of his golden skin.

When my gaze meets his, and I see the sexy smirk, I let out a chuckle. "Don't blame me for staring. You're way too handsome for your own good."

Kao's grin just grows. "My turn." I help him take my shirt off, and while I'm still throwing it to the floor, he's already unsnapping my bra and pulling it off.

My eyes quickly dart to his face, and I watch as his lips part at the sight of my breasts. "Fucking, perfect," he murmurs before he lowers his head and sucks my nipple into the warmth of his mouth.

Oh. God.

Soooo good.

I arch into him, and it makes him scrape his teeth over the hard bud. He pulls back and smiles up at me. "So much better than vegetables."

I let out a burst of laughter, and then Kao's hand covers my breast, and he begins to massage me. "You're a perfect fit."

I bask in the compliment as my hands move to his toned back.

Kao's mouth finds mine, and as the kiss intensifies, his touch grows harder until it makes me feel feverish with want for him.

My hands drop to his ass and gripping him hard, I try to push him down on me. Instead of getting my wish, Kao lifts himself slightly, and his hand leaves my breast. I'm just about to protest when his hand dips under my sweatpants, and I feel his fingers brush over my sensitive flesh.

His lips knead and nip at mine with such fervor, it feels like I'm going to burn up from the heat he creates in me.

Kao spreads me, and the moment his finger brushes over my clit, my body jerks at the sharp sensation of pleasure it causes.

I bring my left hand up to his jaw while I push my right hand under his sweatpants so I can feel his skin as I grip his ass.

Kao breaks the kiss, and his eyes lock on my face. He stares at me with so much concentration, and I'm just about to start feeling awkward when the corner of his mouth lifts, and he whispers, "There you are." I begin to frown, but then he explains, "If I stare long enough, the blurriness fades a little."

His eyes caress my face with so much love it makes a lump swell in my throat. Before I can get emotional, his hand moves down, and he pushes a finger inside me.

My lips part on a silent gasp at the intense feeling of having Kao touch me so intimately for the first time.

I move my hand behind his neck and pull his mouth back to mine as he begins to slowly thrust his finger inside me. When our tongues touch, Kao presses his palm down on my clit, and I moan into his mouth.

His touch grows harder, and when I begin to feel a tightening in my abdomen, I spread my legs wider. Then he stops abruptly, and I let out a frustrated groan.

All I get is a chuckle as Kao breaks the kiss.

KAO

I'm pushing my limits, but needing Fallon, I grab hold of her sweatpants and panties and drag the fabric down her legs.

I watch as her eyes widen when I take off my own sweatpants. Not wanting her to get nervous, I say, "No penetration. I just want to feel you."

She nods quickly. "I'm okay with us having sex, though."

I move back over her, and when I press down on her, and I feel her heat and wetness, my body shudders from the pleasure. "Fuck, so good."

I lower my head to her breast and suck hard on her nipple while my right hand kneads her skin over her waist and ribs. I leave a trail of kisses to her neck as I begin to rub my cock against her pussy.

Fallon's hands move over my back until she reaches my ass again, and her nails dig in as her legs fall open, giving me full access to her.

The temptation almost strips me of all thought and reason, but I manage to cling to my self-control, wanting to make love to her this weekend.

When my gaze settles on her face again, Fallon says, "If you take my virginity now, we can get the uncomfortable part out of the way and enjoy the weekend."

I stare at her as surprise ripples through me, and it takes a moment before I can ask, "Virginity? You're a virgin?"

Fallon lets out a chuckle. "Why does everyone think I've had sex already? Even the girls were shocked when I told them the other day."

"Because you're so fucking gorgeous," I state. "Not that I'm complaining."

God, she's going to be all mine.

I'm filled with incredible pride and honor that I'll be her first.

Fallon raises an eyebrow at me, and when I still don't say anything, she tilts her head. "Yes? No? Now is not the time to overthink things."

A wide smile stretches over my face. "I was enjoying the fact that you're all mine."

"Oh." She brings a hand to my jaw, and being the practical, control freak I love so much, she says, "I'm on the pill. Can we skip the condom? I don't want to lose my virginity with rubber between us."

I let out a silent chuckle. I'm just about to answer her when there's a knock at my door, and it has me shouting, "We're sleeping. Go away!"

Fallon begins to laugh under me.

"Did you take your eye drops?" Noah yells back.

"Yes. Go away."

I hear him laugh, and it only makes Fallon laugh harder.

Glaring at her, I say, "This weekend can't come fast enough."

"Remember your eye shields," Noah yells again.

"Fuck off," I shout before I drop my forehead to Fallon's shoulder.

I finally get her naked, and then this shit happens. With the moment obliterated by Noah, I move off of Fallon and lie down beside her. "I swear, it's like living with a bunch of kids, and we haven't even had sex yet."

Still laughing, Fallon snuggles into my side, and then she begins to draw lazy patterns on my chest. "I bet I can get you back in the mood."

"Oh, yeah?" I grin.

Her hand brushes a hot path down my chest and abs, but then she first stops to caress the V running down from my hips before her fingers wrap around my cock. She pushes her upper body over me, and then her mouth is on mine.

That's all it takes for my cock to recover from the mood-killer Noah caused.

Taking hold of her hip, I push her onto her back and wanting her to orgasm, I drop kisses on her body as I move down. My shoulders force her legs to spread open, and then I press a kiss to her neatly trimmed curls. When my tongue

273

swipes over her clit, I feel her thighs quiver. The taste of Fallon explodes on my tongue, and wanting more of her, I suck hard on her clit until her ass begins to lift off the bed. I stop for a moment to glance up at her, and seeing that she's covered her face with a pillow, a grin tugs at my lips.

I begin to alternate between sucking and licking, and soon Fallon's hips are bucking. When her body tightens, and she begins to shudder, I move my hand to her pussy and massage her clit to make the orgasm last. I press a kiss to her abdomen, and only when she pulls the pillow from her face, gasping for air, do I crawl back up her body and crush my mouth to hers so she can taste herself on my lips.

After Fallon's come down from her orgasm, her hand moves down my side, and she wraps her fingers around my cock again. She slowly begins to stroke me, but wanting her to be comfortable, I move onto my back and pull her half over me.

Fallon grins up at me, and then she tightens her hold on my cock. Pleasure ripples through my body, and unable to stop, my hips begin to thrust into her hand. "So, fucking good," I groan. "Don't stop."

Taking hold of her jaw, I lift her face to mine, and I crush our mouths together.

I feel her breasts pressing against my side and chest, our skin slick with sweat and desire.

Fallon begins to pump my cock faster until I'm gasping into her mouth. "Fuck, I'm going to come all over your hand."

I thrust harder into her fingers, and then my body tightens before pleasure shudders through me.

Chapter 23

FALLON

After we cleaned up, we get dressed, and then I help Kao with his eye drops. I have a silly grin plastered on my face.

My first sexual experience with Kao... with a man, and it was perfect even though we didn't have intercourse.

While we wait between eyedrops, I say, "I wonder if it will be sore." When a frown forms on his brow, I explain, "Intercourse. For the first time."

Kao takes hold of my hips and presses a kiss to my stomach, then he tilts his head back again. "We'll just make sure you're well prepared."

"Hmm." I let out a chuckle. "Like earlier, when you went down on me? For future reference, I loved that twirly thing you did with your tongue."

Kao shakes his head. "There's no doubt you and Jase are family. You have no filter."

"Being direct is the best way," I murmur as I lean over him. "Open your eyes." He does as I ask, and I put in the last drops. "All done."

I sit down next to him and rest my cheek against his shoulder. "I can't wait for this weekend."

"That makes two of us."

When the minute is up, Kao blinks a couple of times, and then we get up. The moment he opens his door, I let out a bark of laughter. "Someone stuck a piece of paper to your door." I yank it off and read, "For the love of God, do not disturb. They're '*sleeping*'. God knows they need to get rid of all that tension."

"Noah!" Kao barks while trying to keep his laughter in. "Did you put the note on my door?"

"It was Jase," he instantly calls back.

"Fucker," we hear Jase mutter. "You didn't hesitate to give me up."

As we walk down the hallway, I hear Noah say, "I'm more scared of Fallon than you."

Walking into the living room, I crumple the paper and throw it at my cousin while muttering, "Little shit."

"Ask Mila, there's nothing little about me," Jase sasses me.

"I don't need to know that," I gasp as I walk to the fridge to get some water.

"I'm bored, and I don't want to study," Jase whines.

"Watch a movie," I say before I take a sip. As I swallow, I hold the bottle out to Kao so he can have some.

"Honestly, I'm tired of being inside," he mutters.

I try to think of something we can do but with the scars, I have no intention of going out in public. "Take Mila on a date."

"Babe?" Jase yells as he gets up from the couch. "Wanna go out for dinner?"

I hear Mila answer, "We can order in. I need to bring Fallon up to date with the work she missed."

"Talking about work," Noah says. "Come sit your ass down. We have a test to study for. The professor said he'd let you do it verbally."

"That's good and bad news," Kao mutters. He hands the water back to me and presses a quick kiss to my lips before he goes to sit with Noah.

I walk down the hallway to where Jase is sulking, and Mila is glaring at him. "Sorry, Jase. Guess you'll have to entertain yourself."

"Ouch." He slaps his hand over his chest. "So cold."

Mila darts back into their room to get her laptop, then comes out and asks, "Want to work in your room?"

"Sure."

Jase walks to Hunter's room while Mila and I slip into mine. We make ourselves comfortable on my bed, and before she can open her laptop, Jade comes to join us. "Jase and Hunter are studying. Let me help."

Hana walks past my open door, then she backtracks and asks, "Did I miss the memo that we're getting together?"

"No," I answer with a burst of laughter. "Mila's helping me catch up with work, and Jade's just chilling. Wanna join us?"

She comes in and shuts the door behind her before climbing on the bed to sit next to Jade. "So? What happened?"

Pretending I don't have a clue what she's referring to, I ask, "With?"

"You and Kao were in his room all afternoon," Jade comments, wagging her eyebrows at me.

"We were sleeping," I tease them, knowing they're dying to hear the details.

"Dammit, woman. Are you still a virgin or not?" Hana snaps.

I shake my head, and their eyes begin to widen, and then I say, "Afraid I'm still one."

"Holy shit," Jade gasps. "Kao has some serious self-control."

"Nothing compared to Jase," Mila mutters. "He almost drove me insane for a month."

"Or is it because you want to wait?" Hana asks, her eyes sharpening on me.

"Oh no, I offered it to him on a golden platter," I quickly put her worries to rest. "It's because we live with a bunch of children."

Mila begins to chuckle. "I told Jase not to put up that note."

"We're going away this weekend," I drop the bomb. My friends stare at me, and it has me explaining, "Kao and I. He's taking me to Rancho Valencia in Rancho Santa Fe."

"I've heard that place is off the charts beautiful," Jade comments.

"Yeah, I've been once with my parents for a long weekend. There's tons to do," Mila adds.

"As if they'll even leave the bedroom," Hana chuckles.

"Whatever we do, I'm sure it will be fun," I say, a mischievous grin on my face. "Honestly, I'm just excited about spending time with Kao."

"Okay, let's get some work done," Mila says, opening her laptop.

KAO

Fallon checks the contents of our weekend bags for what must be the hundredth time.

Taking hold of her arm, I pull her onto my lap where I'm sitting on the bed. "If we forget something, we can just buy it there."

She checks her watch, then asks, "What time is the helicopter coming again?"

A smile curves my lips. "Five."

"That gives us twenty minutes," Fallon mutters, her mind probably racing over her mental list of things to do before we leave.

My phone starts to ring, and as Fallon gets up from my lap, I reach in my pocket for the device. Seeing Dad's name flashing on the screen, I answer, "Hey, Dad."

"Sorry, I didn't call yesterday. I was stuck in a meeting until eleven at night."

"Damn." A frown forms on my forehead. "Is everything okay at work?"

"Yes, it's just the annual budget meeting. How was your doctor's appointment?"

I relax when I hear I don't have to worry about Dad, then answer, "It went well. Dr. Hodgson is happy with the progress I'm making."

"How's your sight?"

In the background, I hear Mom asking, "Is that Kao? Put him on speakerphone." A couple of seconds later, she says, "Hi, sweetie. How are you feeling?"

"I'm much better. If I focus for a bit, the blurring fades a little."

"That's great news," Dad says. He gets excited about every minor step I take forward.

"How's Fallon?" Mom asks.

My gaze darts to Fallon's, and I grin. "She's good. I'm taking her away for the weekend. Speaking of which, we have a helicopter to catch at five."

"Oh good, now we don't have to worry about the two of you on the road. Where are you taking her?" Dad asks.

"Rancho Valencia in Rancho Santa Fe. I booked a villa."

"Aww… my son the romantic. At least I did something right," Mom coos. "I hope you have a wonderful weekend."

Then Dad says, "Don't forget to use protection. I'm too young to be a grandfather."

Fallon lets out a snort, and she quickly covers her mouth.

"Don't worry, Dad," I chuckle. "I have to go. Love you both."

After a chorus of I love you's from my parents, I hang up then shake my head. "Well, that just happened."

"Grab the bags," Fallon chuckles. "I want to get out of the suite and have you all to myself." She walks to the door, then pauses. "We have everything, right?"

"Definitely. You checked a couple of times," I assure her as I pick up the luggage.

"Your eyedrops?"

"Yep."

"Your eye shields?"

"Yes."

"Meds for migraines?"

"Fallon," I stop in front of her and press a kiss to her lips, "Let's go."

"Okay." She lets out a breath, and her eyes scan over the room before she walks out.

God, I love my girl.

We finally leave the suite and walking out of the building, we make our way to the helipad situated next to the security booth by the main gates.

Fallon lets out a happy shriek as she climbs into the helicopter. I load the bags first, then climb aboard. Sitting next to her, we put on our headphones, and then I take her hand and hold it on my thigh.

The pilot announces that we're taking off and when we start to lift my stomach drops. Fallon's smile grows as we get a one hundred and eighty view of the campus before we fly away.

I dare a quick glance out of my window, and seeing the mountains down below, I quickly jerk back.

God, I hate heights.

I turn my face to Fallon and watch as she takes in the view below. Bringing our hands up, I press a kiss to her knuckles.

Thirty minutes later, we descend at Rancho Valencia. Thank God we made it in one piece. Taking off the headsets, I get out first, then help Fallon out. Grabbing our luggage, we begin to walk toward the reception area. A concierge comes rushing toward us and takes the bags from me.

"Welcome to Rancho Valencia, Mr. Reed, Miss Reyes. This way, please."

When he leads us away from the reception area, I ask, "Do you have our key card for the villa?"

"Yes, sir."

Damn, I already love this place, and we've only been here five minutes.

"Has everything been arranged like I asked?" I check with him.

"Yes, sir. Once you're ready, I'll take you to the stalls."

"The stalls?" Fallon asks.

"A surprise," I murmur.

The concierge leads us to a beautiful villa, and opening the front door, he sets our bags down by the couch. "I'll be back in thirty minutes, sir."

"Thank you."

I wait for him to leave, then turn to Fallon. "This place is really beautiful." The white furniture makes the place look spacious and clean, accentuated by wooden beams stretching across the ceiling.

"Right." Fallon grins at me, then says, "Let's look around first."

Taking her hand, I let her lead me through the villa before exploring the immediate outside terrain. Everything is luxurious, and there's a peaceful atmosphere drifting in the air. Even though it's winter, all the plants must be evergreen because we're surrounded by nature and pristine grounds.

Walking back into the villa, I say, "You brought a pair of boots like I asked?"

"Yeah?"

"It's time to put them on."

"Why?" Fallon gives me a mischievous grin.

Shaking my head, I chuckle. "No prying. It's a surprise."

Once Fallon has changed out of her heels, we meet the concierge out front. He leads us to where two horses wait for us, and the moment Fallon sees them, she grabs my arm with both her hands and does a little excited dance.

"Oh my gosh, they're magnificent," Fallon gasps, and she immediately steps closer to them, giving them attention.

The concierge explains which trail we should follow to get to the picnic they have set up for us.

I wait for Fallon to climb on her horse before I get on mine, and once we're both ready, we slowly gallop toward a path that disappears into a lining of trees.

Fallon has a beautiful smile on her face as she glances around, and then she lets out a happy sigh. "You've outdone yourself, Mr. Reed."

"I'm glad you like it." My only mission this weekend is to impress Fallon and to show her how much I love her. The past couple of days, we've been ripping each other's clothes off and just wanting to talk with Fallon, I ask, "How's the school work coming along? Are you all caught up?"

"Yeah, but my accountancy mark dropped to seventy-five. I need to get it back to ninety."

"Noah can help you," I remind her.

"I just have to study hard for the exam next week. I should be fine after that."

There's a moment's silence as our horses leisurely carry us through the greenery and trees, then I ask, "Are you still going to work at CRC during the summer break?"

"Oh, definitely." She lets out a chuckle. "There's no getting out of that."

Fallon will eventually take over as vice president of CRC Holdings, and I'm worried about the pressure she'll be under. "Are you at least looking forward to it?"

"Yeah, and I'll have Jase and Hunter there." Fallon smiles at me. "You're graduating in a couple of months.

Last we spoke about the future, you were in two minds about joining Indie Ink. Have you decided what you're going to do?"

I pull an unsure face. "I've been talking to Noah about it. He was going to take over the design department from Uncle Jax. He's better with numbers than I am, though. We might swap, and Noah can take over the finance side from my dad."

"So, you'll take over from Mr. West then?" Fallon asks. "Honestly, I think that would be a better move for you."

"We still need to talk with our fathers, so until then, I'm not sure what's happening when I graduate."

"It will all work out for the best," Fallon encourages me.

We guide the horses around a bend, and then a beautiful sight greets us.

Fallon gasps, "Oh, Kao, it's so romantic." When we climb off the horses, I tie them to a tree so they can graze. The concierge will come to get them and take them back to their stalls, so there's no hurry for Fallon and me to head back.

The resort has put up a canopy, and white lace gently flutters in the breeze. Pillows are scattered elegantly over the ground, and our dinner is waiting on a table situated in the middle.

With Fallon being under twenty-one, I had them give us non-alcoholic champagne.

I sit down opposite Fallon and grin at her. "I hope you're okay with finger foods. I just want to sit out here for a while and enjoy the evening with you."

"It's perfect." One of the horse's grunts, and then Fallon asks, "Ah, how are we getting back if they're taking the horses?"

"We'll walk. I didn't think it would be wise riding horses in the dark," I explain. Taking the champagne from the ice bucket, I pour us each a glass. Holding mine up, I say, "Here's to us having a weekend alone."

"For the first time," Fallon adds before we each take a sip. The fruity taste is refreshing.

"It's still surreal that we're sitting here," Fallon suddenly admits.

"After everything that's happened?" I ask.

"Not just that." She pauses for a moment. "It feels like it's taken forever for us to get here."

"Sorry I'm so slow," I chuckle.

Fallon places some cheese on a couple of crackers and hands me one, then she says, "When I asked you to the prom, I was kind of hoping you'd get the message that I liked you."

Tilting my head, I reply, "But you asked me as a friend." I begin to frown. "Didn't you?"

She shakes her head and first swallows the bite she took. "I was already head over heels for you back then. You have no idea how happy I was when you said you'd go with me."

Reaching across the table, I place my hand over Fallon's. "We're together now."

"Yeah." A happy smile stretches over her face. "And now is all that matters."

Chapter 24

FALLON

As the sun sets and the sky is filled with brilliant colors, I wish Kao could see it.

We've been gorging ourselves for the past two hours and just talking about everything. I realize this is what I've needed most. Just me and Kao communicating about the important things in our lives.

Kao takes a sip of his champagne, then says, "To think in four months, everything will change again."

A frown forms on my forehead, and I ask, "What do you mean?"

"Jase, Hunter, Noah, and I will be moving out of the suite. I'll have to go house shopping during the summer break."

He pulls a worried face that draws a chuckle from me. Kao hates anything that forces him to interact with people. It has me offering, "I could make you a list of properties you might like?"

Kao's eyebrows pop up. "That would be amazing. Actually, if you love the house, I'll just sign on the dotted line."

"Hmm… that's a lot of trust you're placing in me," I tease him.

"Why? We might as well choose a house we both love because you'll move in eventually," Kao states in such a nonchalant way it has me gaping at him like a fish out of water.

"You want me to live with you?" I ask, still feeling ripples of surprise trickling through me.

"Of course." His mouth curves into a sexy grin. "Or do you plan on dumping my ass any time soon?"

"Not a chance in hell," I grumble. "Next time you try to get rid of me, I'm kidnapping you and tying you to my bed."

I try to make a joke about it, but I still feel embers of hurt smoldering in my heart.

Kao gets up. "Let's move the table to the side so we can lie down. I help him, and once we're comfortable between all the pillows, Kao asks, "Have you forgiven me?"

I turn on my side and rest my cheek on his shoulder. "Yeah, I understand why you pushed me away."

"Still, I hate what I did to you," he murmurs. "But I want you to know, even though I lost my mind, I still loved you. That's the one thing I don't want you to ever doubt." Kao turns, so he's facing me, and he presses a tender kiss to my mouth. "I wish there was a way I could show you how much I love you."

"There is," I murmur while a bubble of happiness forms around us. "Just stay by my side and trust that I'm strong enough to handle whatever life throws at us. Don't make decisions about us by yourself. We're in this together."

Kao brings his hand to my scarred cheek, and for the first time, I don't have the urge to pull away as his fingers brush over my skin. "You're such an amazing woman, Fallon."

My lips curve up. "Only in your eyes."

I curl up against Kao and watch as the stars begin to twinkle in the night sky.

This is the Kao I fell in love with. The man who moves in the shadows and avoids people like the plague, but deep down, he's a hopeless romantic who loves with all his heart.

Even though we were ripped apart, Kao fought his way back to me.

My stubborn hermit.

I let out a chuckle.

"What?" Kao asks.

"We actually fit perfectly together. I'm a neurotic control freak, and you lock down when anything disturbs your routine. With me by your side, your days will be planned years ahead."

Kao pulls me closer and presses his lips to my temple, then he whispers, "That's because you're my soul mate."

I turn my face to his and let my eyes caress his handsome features. "I love you so much. My whole world revolves around you, Kao."

We lie and stare at each other, and every couple of minutes, we steal a tender kiss, quietly enjoying each other.

Time fades into the night, and my heart weaves every dream, every hope, and every day that's left of my life around Kao.

A week ago, I was an empty shell – a ghost of the woman I used to be before the accident. But then Kao came back to me, and he took every broken piece and glued me back together with his gentle nature and profound love.

As we hold hands while walking toward our villa, I'm overcome with emotion and relief that I didn't lose him. No man would ever be able to fill the place Kao has in my heart.

He is my heart. Every single beat.

This past week it feels like I fell in love with him again. Only this time, it's not the teenage crush I had on him, nor the contented emotions I had before the accident. Now I love him fiercely, with a desire that will never burn out.

I'm going to love him every second of every day as if I can lose him at any moment. I'll never take him for granted again.

Kao pulls his hand free from mine then wraps his arm around my shoulders. He pulls me tightly to his side and presses a kiss to my temple.

When we walk into the villa, I come to a sudden halt as a gasp rushes over my parted lips. Lanterns have been lit, and they're scattered around the living room, making it look like a fairyland. Soft music fills the air, and the moment is so emotional it fills my eyes with tears.

Kao shuts the door, and then he pulls me to his chest, and we begin to dance slowly. I wrap my arms around his neck and stare up at his face, my entire being bursting with something that can't possibly just be love. This is more. It feels sacred.

Every song we sway to feels like a promise from Kao.

He lowers his head and softly brushes his lips over mine, then he pulls back an inch. I feel him breathe, and it makes my insides tighten with anticipation. Smelling his woodsy scent, feeling his arms around me, and having his sole focus on me – it makes my heartbeat speed up, and desire burns through me like a wildfire.

When *Ed Sheeran's Perfect* begins to fill the air, Kao's mouth finds mine. It's explosive and consuming, as if he's branding me as his.

My fingers slip into his hair as our tongues dance to the rhythm of the music.

KAO

Kissing Fallon, it feels like I'm a man on my knees, begging her to accept my love.

She can have any man she wants, yet she's standing in my arms. I don't know what I did to deserve her, but I'll never stop thanking the universe for giving her to me.

Breaking the kiss, there's an aching twinge in my chest from how much I love her. I frame her face with my hands. "Everything I am begins and ends with you."

Fallon takes hold of my hand, and then she pulls me out of the living room and up the stairs to the bedroom.

We stop at the foot of the bed, and she turns to face me. The music drifts to us from downstairs as I close the small gap between us. With my eyes on her face, I lift my hands, and I begin to unbutton her blouse. When I push the fabric off her shoulders, and it drops to the floor, I lower my head and press a kiss to the swell of her breast peeking from the lacy bra.

"Give me a second," Fallon murmurs, and then she sits down on the bed to yank off her boots. She gets back up and unbuttoning her jeans, she shoves them down her legs, stepping out of them.

I move forward, and wrapping my arm around her waist, I yank her against me. "I want to undress you."

"Oh… okay."

I pretend to be serious as I ask, "Are you going to let me love you?"

She quickly nods, and it makes the corner of my mouth lift.

Lifting my other hand to her face, I brush her hair back. "You take my breath away."

I press a kiss to her scars before moving to her mouth. I keep the kiss slow, wanting to savor every moment of making love to Fallon.

Moving my arm that's around her waist up her back, I unclasp her bra. Pulling the lace off of her, I let it fall to the floor. Breaking the kiss, I bring my hand to the swell of her breast as I look down.

With my sight still stuck in black and white and the blurring, it feels like I'm caught in a movie from the early nineteen hundreds. For some weird reason, I can't explain, it makes this moment more profound. I'm focused on how soft and feminine Fallon feels beneath my hands, the sound of her breaths rushing over her lips, the heat coming from her body.

I brush my thumb over her nipple, and feeling her skin pebble makes me achingly hard for her.

I brush my palm down her ribs and trim waistline. Lowering myself, I go down on one knee, and I take hold of her panties, slowly pulling them down her legs. It feels like I'm unwrapping the greatest gift of my life.

I press a kiss to her thigh, then to her hip before I climb back to my feet.

"You're really good at this," she whispers. "You have me all naked while you're still fully clothed." Fallon lifts her hands to my shirt, and she begins to undo the buttons. "It's my turn now."

I keep still as she undresses me, and when we're both naked, I close the distance between us, and pressing my body to Fallon's, I crush my mouth to hers. Lifting my hands, I frame her face as I tilt my head, and I pour all my desire and love into the kiss.

Fallon grabs hold of my forearms for a moment, but then she wraps her arms around me, and her nails dig into my back.

Pushing against her with my body, I force her toward the bed. We pull apart as Fallon slides onto the mattress, but I follow her and our mouths fuse together again.

I lie down, only half my body covering hers, placing my right hand on her hip. Our tongues keep dancing, and it feels like I'm getting drunk on the taste of her. My breaths come faster, and my heart is thundering against my ribs as the moment grows with intensity.

I slide my hand down and softly brush my knuckles over her pussy. When I massage her a little harder, her

299

breaths burst into my mouth. I focus on her clit and circling her opening. Her hips begin to move, and she grinds herself against my hand. I pull my mouth away from hers and pressing kisses to her skin, I move down her body until my tongue flicks over her clit. A moan drifts from Fallon and wanting her to orgasm, I begin to alternate between sucking hard and thrusting my tongue inside her pussy.

"God. Kao," she cries, then her body stiffens before she shudders as she finds her release. A sound slips over her lips, sounding like something caught between a gasp and a low moan, and it drives me wild.

I crawl up her body and positioning my cock at her entrance, I pause to stare down at her. I will my eyes to stop blurring for a moment just so I can see her face clearly as I enter her for the first time.

Bringing her hand to my jaw, she whispers, "What's wrong?"

I keep staring until her face comes more into focus. "Nothing. I just want to look at you."

There isn't a word to describe what I feel for Fallon. I press a tender kiss to her mouth, and bracing my arms on either side of her head, I begin to push into her.

Her breath bursts over my lips, and bringing her hands up, she takes hold of the back of my shoulders.

"I love you, Fallon," I say, my voice filled with the wonder I'm experiencing as I push deeper inside her. When she stiffens, I pause so she can adjust to me. I feel her relax again and do my best to enter her slowly. By the time I'm entirely inside her, my body trembles from having to hold back.

Knowing I've just taken Fallon's virginity fills me with complete awe. I press a kiss to her mouth, but then I feel her lips quiver beneath mine.

"Did I hurt you?" the words explode from me as worry pours through my veins.

Fallon quickly shakes her head. "No. I'm just emotional because we're finally together like this," she whispers.

I press another kiss to her lips, and then I pull out. Thrusting back inside Fallon, my eyes drift shut from the intense pleasure rushing through my body.

Chapter 25

FALLON

The expression on Kao's face as he thrusts into me is...
nothing short of erotic. It's a complete sensory overload.

Finally, having Kao inside me after loving him for so
long is surreal. Every time he pushes back into me, I feel
his cock massage my inner walls, and it sends tingles
shooting through my body like fireworks. Lifting my head,
I claim his parted lips and mimic his movements with my
tongue. My hands caress the broad expanse of his back,
memorizing every rippling muscle.

Kao takes control of the kiss, and he begins to thrust
harder and faster. I wrap my legs over his ass and hold onto
him as my abdomen begins to tighten again.

"Fuck," Kao gasps into my mouth. He lowers his head
and presses his lips to the scars on my neck as he sinks
deep inside me. Knowing he's caught up in ecstasy tells me
all I need to know – Kao really doesn't care about the
marks on my face and neck.

I tighten my arms around him and bury my face in his neck. The sound of our skin coming together and our breaths racing over our lips makes my insides tighten, and then pleasure rolls over me like waves lapping at the shore.

I let out a whimpering moan as my orgasm shudders through me. Kao begins to jerk, and his cock slams deep into me, making residual pleasure pulse in me.

When Kao finds his release with a soft grunt, he pushes his arms under me and grips me tightly to his chest.

Coming down from our orgasms, Kao doesn't move off of me. He keeps pressing tender kisses to my neck, working his way up to my cheek before he stops to stare down at me.

I begin to draw lazy patterns on his back, soaking up the last couple of moments of us being one.

"You complete me in every way," Kao whispers.

My mouth curves up, and lifting my head, I kiss him before I murmur, "You are the only man I'll ever love. No one will be able to measure up to the high standards you've set."

Waking up in Kao's arms is nothing short of blissful. I snuggle against his strong body and let out a contented sigh.

"Morning, beautiful," Kao murmurs, his voice low and hoarse with sleep.

"Morning." Lifting my head, I press a kiss to his jaw, and then I pull away, climbing out of bed. I walk to the windows and opening the curtains, I look at the sunny day awaiting us. Turning back to the bed, I say, "Time to get up. I'm starving."

"Yeah, let me feed my woman," Kao teases as he throws the covers back.

I pull on a red long sleeve shirt and a pair of black pants, opting for boots instead of my usual heels, just in case Kao wants to go for a walk after breakfast.

When I walk into the bathroom, and I see Kao squirting toothpaste on the toothbrush, my eyes widen. "Can you see what you're doing?"

Kao pauses, and then realization flashes over his face. "Shit, I can see it."

"Oh, my God!" I let out a happy shriek and rush to hug him from behind. "We have to celebrate."

Kao drops the toothbrush and toothpaste in the sink, and he spins around, a shocked expression on his face. "Fallon, I can see red."

Seeing the relief and amazement on Kao's face makes tears jump to my eyes.

Lifting myself on my tiptoes, I press a kiss to his mouth. "It's only a matter of time now before you'll see clearly again."

A burst of laughter explodes over Kao's lips, and wrapping his arms around me, he lifts me against his body and hugs the crap out of me. I wrap my arms around his neck, and thankful tears escape my eyes.

KAO

Holy shit. I can't describe how I feel right now. I want to laugh and cry. I want to shout my relief to the heavens and fall to my knees with absolute gratefulness.

I cling to Fallon, and when I manage to regain control over my emotions, I set her down on her feet and then push her back so I can look at her top again.

"Red is officially my favorite color," I chuckle.

"Thankfully, I have a couple of red items I can wear for you," Fallon teases me. She hugs me again. "Now, this weekend is perfect."

We brush our teeth like an old married couple while grinning at each other in the mirror's reflection.

The thought gets stuck in my mind.

I want to marry Fallon. I don't want to spend a day apart from her.

"What?" Fallon mumbles around her toothbrush.

I rinse my mouth out, then say, "I'm just happy."

As soon as we're ready, I take Fallon's hand and weave my fingers with hers. We leave the villa and leisurely make our way over to the restaurant. Fallon picks a table that looks out over a pond. She grabs a menu and begins to read the dishes to me, making my lips curve up.

"Pancakes," I blurt out before she reads the whole list of food to me.

"Hmm, and bacon," she adds. She places our orders and also asks for two cappuccinos and freshly squeezed orange juice.

When the waiter leaves, Fallon grins at me. "I love this place. Thank you for bringing me."

Smiling, I say, "We should make time to come here at least once a year."

"That would be awesome," she agrees. "We can make it our New Years' getaway."

"I like the sound of that."

We don't have to wait long for our food, and my tastebuds are in heaven from how fluffy and full of flavor the pancakes are.

I cut off a piece and feed Fallon, then I watch as she lets out an orgasmic-worthy groan. "So good."

"You have no idea," I mumble under my breath.

After breakfast, we walk in a random direction. We don't take in much of the immaculate grounds because we're too busy stealing smiles from each other.

"What does your dream house look like?" I ask as we follow a path.

"As long as it's big enough for you, me, two kids, and a couple of dogs, I'll be happy."

"Only two?" I ask, pretending to be shocked.

"Yeah, unless you plan on giving birth," she sasses me.

"I'm good with two." My quick reply draws a chuckle from her.

"I'd like something we can fix up. A house we can make our own. I guess I'll only know once I see it," Fallon explains. "I also want a sunroom like my Aunt Jamie has. It's the perfect room to curl up with a book."

"And huge bay windows for light to come in," I begin to weave my dream with hers.

Fallon grips my hand tightly, and there's excitement in her voice as she says, "Yes, and I really like white furniture, like in the villa."

"And wooden beams over the ceiling," I add.

"God, now I want to go house shopping," Fallon says, her excitement coming off her in waves.

Spotting a bench, I gesture to it. "Want to sit for a while?"

"Yeah."

When we take a seat, I drape my left arm over Fallon's shoulders and ask, "So two kids. A boy and girl?"

"That would be ideal, but it's not like we can place an order."

"Okay, if we're lucky and we have a boy and a girl, what do you want to name them?"

Fallon crosses her legs and turns her body into me. She takes hold of my right hand and begins to follow the map of veins running up my forearm with her pointer finger. "For a boy, I like Asher, and for a girl..." she pauses to think about it, then says, "Emery." She glances up at me. "What are your favorite names?"

"Hmm…" I think about it for a while, then answer, "I like Asher for a boy. But I really want to name my daughter, Summer."

Fallon smiles at me. "After your aunt?"

"Yeah," I murmur.

The tragedy which took her life is a dark secret only those closest to my family know about. My dad almost died when my grandfather shot his whole family before turning the gun on himself.

"Then we'll name our daughter Summer," Fallon says before pressing a kiss to my mouth.

"Our daughter," I whisper as she pulls back. "I love the sound of that."

"Let's just wait a couple of years, though." Fallon grins, then she teases me, "Your dad's too young to be a grandfather."

I let out a bark of laughter and hug her to my side.

Chapter 26

FALLON

When we get back to Trinity late Sunday afternoon, I feel like a new woman. The weekend away with Kao was a dream come true and what we needed to put the past month behind us. I feel secure in our love and relationship, and all the doubt I had after the accident has faded away.

After we've unpacked our weekend bags, Kao and I go sit in the living room. He picks up my legs and drapes them over his lap, and then he wraps his arms around me. I snuggle into his chest and let out a happy sigh. "The weekend was amazing. Thank you."

He presses a kiss to the top of my head, and I feel his breaths stirring my hair. "I wish we could stay there, but responsibilities call."

I let out a soft chuckle. "Dang those pesky responsibilities."

Kao's arms grip me tighter for a moment, and then he says, "I checked with Summer, and the decorating committee is meeting tomorrow morning at seven." I glance up at him, still apprehensive about being active around campus with the scars. Kao gives me an encouraging smile. "I'll go with you. Like I said, you can even put me to work."

I know it's important I resume doing the things I love, but...

"Just one meeting. If it doesn't go well, I'll stop pushing," Kao tries again.

Not wanting to disappoint him, I nod. "Okay. One meeting."

A smile stretches over his face. "Thank you."

I lift my face and press a kiss to his lips.

"You're back," Jase says as he comes to plop down on one of the couches. "How was your trip?"

"So good," I grin. "You should take Mila there. She'd love it."

Jase's gaze sharpens on us, and a pleased look settles on his face. "You both owe me a bottle of whiskey."

Frowning, I ask, "Why?"

"For playing cupid to your stubborn assess." He gets up and walking to the hallway, he says, "Glad to see you both happy."

"Thanks, Jase," I call after him.

Kao lets out a chuckle. "I'll get him a thank you gift from us."

I'm anxious as Kao walks with me to the office space I had converted for the decorating committee to meet and prepare for events.

Entering the administration building, my stomach tightens with knots. I'm scared one of the girls will see the scars. I don't want someone's horrified reaction ruining the little progress I've made, and it's only two weeks until my surgery.

Kao tightens his hold on my hand, and leaning closer, he says, "I'm proud of you."

I give him a nervous smile right before we walk into the room.

"Fallon!" Summer shrieks, and she rushes over to give me a hug. "I'm so glad you decided to come." She pulls me away from Kao to a table where we do all our planning. "I was just about to cry. With you gone, some of the girls got out of control, and they wanted to take over. It was a mess."

My gaze moves over the table, and I frown, "Silk hearts? Seriously? They'll be all droopy." I begin to remove everything that won't work, then grumble, "You'd freaking think we were planning a junior prom. What the hell?"

"Exactly," Summer whines. "It was a nightmare."

Suddenly she throws her arms around my neck and hugs me again. "I'm so glad you're back."

When she pulls back, I give her a reassuring smile. "Don't worry, we'll get it under control again."

I glance to where Kao's grabbed some coffee. He's leaning against the wall, watching me with a proud smile on his face.

The rest of the girls arrive, and when they see me, they all take a turn to hug me. They all shoot Kao a curious look, and it has him moving to the back of the room.

Kao being here, even though he struggles to be around people, shows me how much he loves me.

Wanting to draw everyone's attention away from him, I say, "Let's start the meeting." I plug my laptop into the overhead projector. When an image of various heart-shaped lanterns appears on the screen, I say, "This is the theme we're going with. The traditional red heart theme is overdone. We're going with light and hearts this year."

Once I have the girls' attention, we begin discussing all the various aspects of the ball. By the time the meeting comes to a close, I feel more confident.

Kao was right. I have to continue doing the things I love.

As I unplug my laptop and place it back in my bag, Kao comes to stand next to me. "Admit it, you enjoyed that," he teases me.

"Hmm…" I pull an unsure face, "maybe a little."

Kao takes my bag so he can carry it, and then his arm wraps around my waist, and he pulls me in for a kiss.

When we pull apart, one of the girls asks, "Are you guys official now?"

Grinning, I nod while joking with them, "Yeah, so hands off my man."

Summer is the only one who says, "I'm happy for you both."

She used to hang out with two girls I couldn't stand, but after they left Trinity, Summer has become a friend and a great asset to the decorating committee.

Kao's fingers intertwine with mine, and he begins to drag me out of the room, saying, "It's time to feed your man."

KAO

Over the past two weeks, my sight has gotten much better. I'm able to see all the primary colors but still struggle with shades. The blurriness has lessened somewhat, and I'm hoping in another two to four weeks, my sight will be back to what it was before the accident.

The main thing I'm focusing on is that my vision keeps improving.

Fallon checks the time again, and it has me taking hold of her arm. I pull her against my chest and wrap her up in a hug. "Everything is going to go well," I try to reassure her.

Wrapping her arms around my waist, she sucks in a deep breath. "I'm just scared."

"I'll be there every step of the way." Pulling her a little back, I press a tender kiss to her lips and getting to make out the rich golden-brown of her irises, a smile tugs at my mouth. "We're in this together. Okay?"

Fallon nods, and she gives me a quick hug before she pulls back and linking our hands, we leave the room.

When we walk into the shared open space, Noah glances up from where he's drinking coffee, "Are you guys leaving?"

"Yeah, Fallon needs to check-in by seven."

He sets down his cup and comes to give her a hug. "Good luck, Fallon."

"Thanks."

As we take a step toward the front door, Hana calls out, "Hold your horses." She comes to join us, then says, "Did you think I'd let you leave without me?"

A wide smile splits over Fallon's face. "Of course not, but I wanted you to sleep in."

"Not a chance in hell of that happening."

Fallon, Hana, and I file out of the suite. While we make our way out of the building, Fallon says, "Thank you for coming with, Hana."

"Of course. There's nowhere else I'd rather be."

When Fallon unlocks the car, Hana climbs in the back, and I slip into the passenger side. Fallon gives me a nervous smile. We first put on our seat belts, then I lean over and give her a kiss.

I'll only be able to drive once my doctor clears me. Dad's already gotten me another car, seeing as my old one was written off. Then again, I'm not sure I'm ready to be behind a steering wheel. That's something I'll face once Fallon is better.

When Fallon parks the car outside the hospital, she lets out a heavy breath. "Ugh, I'm so nervous. I feel nauseous."

"You'll be fine," Hana says before she climbs out of the vehicle.

It's a process of checking Fallon into the hospital, and when we finally get shown to a private room, Hana says, "I'm going to get us some coffee." She rushes out of the room, probably to give us some privacy.

I bring my hands to Fallon's face and framing her cheeks, I stare deep into her eyes. "Who loves you?"

She begins to grin as she looks up at me. "You."

"And who am I?"

Her grin widens into a smile, "Mine."

"Damn right," I chuckle, then growing serious, I say. "You're going to be fine. Okay? Dr. Menard is the best."

Fallon nods, looking a little less tense.

I lean down, and moving my left hand out of the way, I press kisses to her scars. A nurse comes in, and I pull back so she can take Fallon's vitals. Once she's done, the nurse says, "Dr. Menard has been notified that you're here. He'll be with you shortly."

Once the nurse leaves, Fallon sits down on the bed.

317

When Hana comes back into the room, she hands me a coffee.

"Thanks."

Hana takes a sip of her own, then her eyes lock on mine.

"What?"

A smile tugs at Hana's lips. "Thanks, Kao."

Frowning, I ask, "For?"

"Being the man Fallon deserves."

A grin spreads over my face. Before I can think of something to say, Fallon chuckles. "Yeah, he's the best, isn't he?" Then she glares at our coffees. "So unfair that I can't have any."

"Sorry, but I'll turn into a serial killer if I don't get caffeine in," Hana jokes.

Just then, Mr. and Mrs. Reyes comes in. They hug Fallon and greet us before Mr. Reyes asks, "Has Dr. Menard been to see you?"

"The nurse said he'll be here soon," Fallon answers.

Fallon sits down on the bed but shoots back up when Dr. Menard comes in.

He first greets everyone, then turns to Fallon, "How's my patient today? Nervous?"

"A minute away from a nervous breakdown," Fallon admits. "It's good to see you again, Doctor."

"Don't worry," Dr. Menard says, a reassuring smile on his face. "When I'm done, you'll be good as new. Sit so I can take a look."

I move closer and watch as he inspects the scars. "I'll be able to remove most of them." His finger traces over the scar stretching from Fallon's ear to her neck. "This sucker might be a bit tricky. You might be left with a faint scar, but we can treat it afterward."

A hopeful expression crosses Fallon's features. "So there's a chance I won't be left with any scars?"

Dr. Menard gives her a comforting look. "I'll do my best." He checks the time. "I'll see you in thirty minutes. Okay?" Giving her shoulder a squeeze, he smiles. "Try not to worry too much."

"Okay." Fallon lets out a deep breath.

When Dr. Menard leaves, I grin at Fallon. "Do you feel better?"

She nods. "He seems confident, right?"

"Yeah, I'm sure he'll remove all the scars," I reassure her.

"God, I hope so," she breathes.

"Kao's right," Mr. Reyes agrees. He gives Fallon's arm a squeeze. "This will all be over soon."

"Thanks, Daddy."

I go to sit down next to Fallon and take hold of her hand. Leaning over, I press a kiss to her temple.

Mr. Reyes' eyes lock with mine, and I see the questions in them. I'll need to make an appointment to see him to explain I'm dating his daughter.

Hopefully, he won't kill me.

Turning my focus back to Fallon, I try to remain positive for her. God, I don't know what I'll do if Dr. Menard is unable to remove all the scars. Fallon won't handle it well.

Whatever happens, I'll be there for her.

Chapter 27

FALLON

Coming to, I feel groggy and nauseous. I let out a confused groan.

"Hey, beautiful," I hear Kao murmur. I feel him press a kiss to my forehead.

Prying my eyes open, my sight settles on Kao's face. "Is it over?" I grumble, still half out of it.

"Yeah, Dr. Menard will be here shortly, but he said the surgery went well."

"He did?" Lifting a hand, I take hold of Kao's arm as he leans over me, and then I drift off again.

"Fallon," I hear someone say. "Time to wake up."

I pry my eyes open and see Dr. Menard smile down at me.

"Hi, Doctor," I mutter, still half asleep.

"How do you feel?"

I sit up in the bed as my head clears of the fog still left over from the anesthetic. "Ah... okay."

"No pain?"

"No."

Dr. Menard gestures to my face and neck. "The surgery went well. I've cut out the keloid scar and stitched your skin back nicely. I made sure there's no tension, and I'm confident it will heal beautifully."

"Really?" I ask as hope bursts in my chest, leaving me feeling overemotional.

"Once you feel better, you can go home. A nurse will give you some painkillers to manage any discomfort you may feel. Also, keep the dressings in place until I see you in three days for your post-op visit."

"Thank you." My eyes follow Dr. Menard as he leaves, my heart still too afraid to let hope in. I think once I see my face and the scars are gone, only then I'll be able to relax.

Dad comes to press a kiss to my forehead, then says, "Don't stress when you see the dressings, it's just to cover the stitches. Okay?"

My dad knows me well.

I lift my hand and softly brush my fingertips over the bandages. "They're not as padded this time."

"Yeah, it's just to protect the stitches," Dad assures me.

My eyes drift from Dad to Mom, then to Hana. Finally, my gaze settles on Kao. He's keeping to the side, probably so my parents can fuss over me.

Turning my eyes back to Dad, I say, "I feel good. Can you get a nurse so I can check out?"

"Sure." Dad immediately leaves.

I throw the covers back and swing my legs off the bed, and let out a deep breath. "I'm glad the surgery is over."

Mom takes a brush from her bag and comes to fix my hair. When she's done, she smiles lovingly at me.

Once we're back at the suite, I go to shower the hospital smell off. After drying myself and putting on a pair of sweatpants and a t-shirt, I stop to look at my reflection in the mirror.

There is white tape stuck over the stitches, which in my opinion, look a million times better than the red, swollen, and jagged scars.

When I step out of the bathroom, I see Kao lying on my bed. His eyes are closed, and wondering if he fell asleep, I carefully crawl onto the bed. I press a kiss to his lips, and when I pull back, his blue gaze locks on mine.

"All clean," I whisper. "Do you want to sleep?"

Kao pulls me down, and I snuggle into his body. "Hmm… it was an eventful day."

Lifting my head, I kiss him again. "Thank you for coming with me."

"Where you go, I go," he murmurs before he claims my mouth in a deep kiss. Before I can get carried away and undress him, Kao pulls back. "No sexy times. I want those stitches to heal properly."

I frown up at him. "So no sex until they come out?"

Kao chuckles. "Just three days until after you've seen Dr. Menard for your post-op visit."

"But there will be kissing?" I ask, grinning at him.

"For sure." His lips lock on mine, and we lie and make out for a couple of minutes before we call it a night.

KAO

My nerves feel like they've been put through a shredder by the time I knock on the front door. Noah dropped me off a couple of seconds ago. With his help, I managed to get out of the suite with the excuse Noah and I were visiting his parents.

The front door opens, and I come face to face with Fallon's dad. Instantly his eyes sharpen on me. "Kao. Come in."

"Evening, sir." I step inside and then follow him to the living room.

"Take a seat," Mr. Reyes says, then he pins me with a frown. "Why did you want to see me?"

Taking a deep breath, I clasp my hands together while resting my forearms on my knees. "It's about Fallon."

His facial expression remains stoic.

"I thought you should know I'm dating your daughter."

"I gathered as much," he grumbles.

"I love her," the words burst over my lips, needing him to know I'm serious about her.

Mr. Reyes tilts his head, his eyes narrowing on me. "You broke her heart."

"I was trying to protect her," I begin to explain.

When I pause, trying to gather my thoughts, Mr. Reyes snaps, "From what, Kao?"

"Myself." I lock eyes with Mr. Reyes. "I didn't want to tie her down to a blind man."

Only then does he relax a little. "I can understand that, but the way you went about it sucked ass."

"Totally agree," I reply, feeling a little less tense.

"Now that you have your sight back, what do you have to offer my daughter?"

"Besides the financial side of things, which I'm sure you know better than me, I only have my love for her. I can promise I'll never hurt her again. I'll protect her with my life. I want to give her the life she deserves."

Mr. Reyes begins to frown again. "This sounds suspiciously like you're about to ask for my blessing."

God, not the way I saw this conversation going.

Clearing my throat, I lift my chin. "I am."

"Well, in that case, you need to give me a moment."

I watch as Mr. Reyes takes his phone from his pocket, and for a second, I worry he's going to call Fallon, but then I hear him say, "Mason, get your ass over here." He dials another number. "Need you here." A moment later. "I don't care if you're having dinner, Lake. Get your ass over to my house right now."

Fuck.

Ooooh fuck.

With Hunter and Hana's father's coming over, I know I'm in deep shit.

When Mr. Reyes is done making the calls to his best friends, he gets up and pours two tumblers of whiskey. Holding one out to me, he says, "You're going to need it."

A couple of minutes later, Mr. Chargill and Mr. Cutler arrive, and as soon as my eyes land on Mr. Chargill, I hide a burst of laughter behind a fake cough. I wish I could take a photo so Hunter can see what his dad looks like right now.

"Mason, what the fuck are you wearing?" Mr. Reyes asks.

I take in the winter pajamas, a robe, and slippers.

"This is the shit Kingsley makes me wear to bed." Mr. Chargill glares at Mr. Cutler when he begins to laugh. "You asking for a beating? It's not like I had time to change. Falcon said it was an emergency."

"I didn't. I said to get your ass over here," Mr. Reyes argues.

"Could've fucking fooled me," Mr. Chargill grumbles.

Mr. Cutler comes to shake my hand. "How are you, Kao?"

"Much better, sir. Thanks for asking."

Mr. Chargill's eyes lock on me. "Your dad says your sight is recovering well?"

"Yes, sir."

"That's good to hear." Mr. Chargill turns his attention to Mr. Reyes. "So, why are we here?"

Mr. Reyes gestures to me. "Kao's about to ask us something."

"Oh?" Mr. Cutler smiles at me. "What do you need."

God have mercy on my soul if they end up killing me.

After sending up the quick prayer, I climb to my feet. I don't know who to look at, so I settle on making eye-contact with Mr. Reyes. "I'd like your blessing." I suck in a deep breath. "I'm going to ask Fallon to marry me."

"Ooooh." Mr. Cutler's eyes widen, and then they shoot to Mr. Reyes.

Mr. Chargill is the first to respond. "You don't think you're both a bit young?"

I quickly shake my head. "I love her. Whether we get married now or in ten years, nothing's going to change how I feel about her. I'm graduating in a couple of months, and we've talked about getting a house."

"You have?" Mr. Reyes murmurs, way too calm for my liking.

"Yes, sir." I swallow hard on the nerves that are grinding my gut to dust.

Mr. Chargill takes a seat on one of the couches. "I have one question."

When Mr. Reyes sits down, I take a seat again next to Mr. Cutler.

Mr. Chargill tilts his head, and he pins me with a deadly stare. "Where were you this past Christmas break?" He shakes his head. "My goddaughter was in a world of pain, and I don't recall seeing you offering her any comfort."

I take in a deep breath, and after gathering my thoughts, I say, "I agree, I didn't handle the situation well. Not at all. When I woke up, and I couldn't see anything, I panicked." Remember the fear and anger, I clasp my hands together. "When I learned Fallon got hurt, I lost it. I blamed myself, and I couldn't live with the fact that I scarred the woman I love more than life itself."

"I went to visit the accident scene," Mr. Reyes interrupts me. "I also saw the dashcam footage."

Dad mentioned it to me, but back then, I couldn't see shit, so I forgot about the footage.

Mr. Reyes gets up. "I have the footage here if you'd like to see it."

I don't know where he's going with this, so all I can do is nod.

I wait as Mr. Reyes switches on the TV, and then he connects his phone to it. A moment later, the screen lights up, and it shows the road we were driving on.

Instantly my muscles tighten.

'Never,' I hear myself say. *'You'll always be beautiful to me.'*

Then Fallon's voice sounds up, *'Even when I'm old and wrinkly?'*

I see the truck coming down the road at one hell of a speed, and my body goes ice cold as it heads right for us.

Christ.

'Shit,' I hear the panic in my voice, and then the nose of my car swerves sharply to the right, and the next second, the sound of the truck slamming into my side of the vehicle vibrates through my body. The car rolls, and then it's pushed into the field next to the road.

'Starting 9-1-1 —'

Mr. Reyes stops the footage, then looks at me. "Four seconds. That's how much time you had to react, and you managed to turn the car so it wouldn't be a head-on collision which could've killed you both." His eyes lock on mine. "You took the full brunt of that hit, and it could've killed you. Still, you didn't hesitate."

"You have my blessing," Mr. Cutler murmurs from next to me. "I know Fallon will be safe with you."

"So," Mr. Reyes says, "You pushed Fallon away because you felt guilty and you were blind?"

"Yes, sir."

"Have you groveled to Fallon," Mr. Chargill asks, a smirk pulling at his mouth.

I let out a chuckle. "Quite a bit, but I'm not done groveling yet."

"Kao," Mr. Reyes says to get my attention, "Can you promise to give my daughter the quality of life I've given her?"

"I'll always do my best to try and measure up to the standard you've set in her life," I answer, meaning every word because I know how important Fallon's parents are to her.

"Well then," Mr. Reyes climbs to his feet, and I instantly shoot up off the couch. He holds his hand out to me, "you have my blessing."

"Wait? That's it?" Mr. Chargill interrupts us. "Am I the only one worried that they're too young?"

"Shut up, Mace," Mr. Cutler snaps. "You proposed to Kingsley when she was nineteen."

"Fuck," Mr. Chargill grumbles. "It's just... Fallon's one of our little girls."

Emotion washes over all their faces. Wanting to reassure them, I say, "Fallon's my life. I'll never stop working my ass off to deserve her."

"You better," Mr. Chargill grumbles.

"So…" Mr. Reyes asks him.

"So what?"

"Does Kao have your blessing?" Mr. Reyes asks, a little exasperated.

"Oh. I guess so. The two of you already outvoted me."

"God, I pity the man who has to ask you for Aria's hand in marriage," Mr. Cutler mumbles.

"You better have the paramedics on standby that day," Mr. Chargill says.

"For you having a heart attack or you beating the poor guy into a coma?" Mr. Reyes asks.

"Probably both."

I struggle to keep the laughter in, just thankful I'm not the poor guy.

Chapter 28

FALLON

I cling to Kao's hand as we walk into Dr. Menard's office. My heart is nothing but a fearful echo behind my ribs.

As we reach reception, the lady smiles up at us. "Fallon Reyes?"

"Yes."

"You can go through. Dr. Menard is waiting for you."

"Thank you." I'm a second away from squeezing the life out of Kao's poor hand as we walk down the short hallway.

When we enter the room, Dr. Menard gets up from where he was sitting behind a desk. He gestures to an adjoining room. "Through there."

We step into the examination room, and I go take a seat.

Dr. Menard comes to stand on my right and smiles down at me. "Are you ready?"

No.

Not in the least.

I nod. "Yeah."

Kao crosses his arms over his chest, and his eyes are locked on mine as Dr. Menard pulls the tape from the stitches.

I hear Dr. Menard breathe as he looks closely at the sutures. "Oooh, yes, they're healing beautifully." He stands back to make eye-contact. "I'm going to remove the stitches. You might feel some discomfort. Okay?"

"Okay?" I suck in a deep breath, and unable to stop myself, my hand reaches for Kao. He darts to my left and grips my fingers tightly with his.

I shut my eyes tightly while Dr. Menard goes to work on my face and neck. My stomach tightens horribly.

After a while, Dr. Menard's fingers brush over my cheek and neck. "I'm very happy. Like I said, we'll do some laser therapy to minimize the scarring even more."

Slowly, I open my eyes. Dr. Menard holds something behind his back as he asks, "Are you ready?"

I'll never be ready.

Kao moves closer to me, placing his other hand on my shoulder.

"Nervous?" Dr. Menard asks. "Trust me. You'll be happy."

Then he brings a mirror from behind his back, and the next second I'm staring at my reflection.

Before my eyes can even focus, a sob bursts from me. Emotion tears through me, and I have to blink rapidly to see my skin.

There are no angry gashes. No haphazard tears.

There's only one thin line running along my jaw that's pink in color.

"The laser therapy will take care of that little sucker," Dr. Menard reminds me.

I bring my trembling right hand to my face and brush my fingers over the soft skin.

"I don't know how you did it, but..." my voice disappears. I have to swallow a couple of times before I can say, "Thank you so much."

God, even if the thin scar remains, I can live with that.

"Great. We'll schedule the laser therapy for next week."

"Okay." I finally manage to smile at the doctor who saved me from a life as a scarred woman.

Dr. Menard looks at Kao. "I think you should take this beautiful woman out for a night on the town."

"Definitely," Kao agrees, a broad smile on his face.

I'm bursting with gratefulness as we leave Dr. Menard, and once we step outside the building, I turn and throw my arms around Kao's neck. His arms instantly wrap around me, and lifting me off my feet, he hugs me tightly.

"God, I'm so relieved," I whisper in his ear.

Kao presses a kiss to the side of my head, and when he begins to walk toward the car, still holding me against his body, I let out a burst of laughter.

Reaching the car, he finally sets me down on my feet, then he frames my face, his touch gentle, and he presses a tender kiss to my mouth.

Kao pulls back, and his eyes lock on mine. "Who loves you?"

"You," I grin at him, loving when he asks me that question. It's become our special thing we do.

"And who am I?"

Not hesitating, I answer, "Mine."

KAO

Dr. Hodgson has cleared me to drive, and honestly, as I stare at the brand new Aston Martin, my heart is thundering against my ribs.

"Come on," Dad says as he holds the key out to me. "You have to get behind the wheel at some point. The sooner, the better."

I take the key from Dad and pressing the button, the doors unlock.

Dad climbs into the passenger side, then calls, "Get your ass in the car, Kao."

Sucking in a deep breath of air, I climb in behind the steering wheel. After we've put on our seat belts, I freeze.

Dad places his hand on my shoulder. "I'm right here. You're going to be fine. Start the car."

I notice my hand is shaking as I press the button.

"Now put it in gear," Dad instructs me.

Pushing the clutch in, I put the car in drive.

Christ.

Closing my eyes, I try to breathe through the panic, tightening my chest.

"You're doing great," Dad murmurs as he rubs my shoulder. "Just one mile. That's all you have to drive."

I nod, and opening my eyes, they scan over the empty stretch of road.

I can do this.

I place my hands on the steering wheel and then let the car slowly roll forward.

"Will you look at that?" Dad chuckles. "We're moving."

I let out a nervous laugh. "You're not helping."

Slowly I pick up speed, and then Dad says, "Seeing as we passed the mile marker and we're still going, you might as well take your old man for a drive."

My confidence grows with every mile that falls behind us, and I steer us in the direction of the beach.

By the time I park the car, and we look out over the ocean, the apprehension I felt is gone.

"Thanks, Dad," I murmur.

"You're welcome." He grins at me. "So, do you love her?"

"Oh yeah, thanks for the car as well."

Dad shakes his head. "I meant Fallon."

I let out a chuckle. "With all my heart." I turn slightly in the seat so I can look at Dad as I say, "I'm going to ask her to marry me."

Dad's eyebrows pop up. "Wow, aren't you full of surprises?"

"I've already spoken to Mr. Reyes."

His eyebrows lift even higher. "How did that go?"

I let out a heavy sigh and shake my head, and when Dad begins to frown, I say, "I got his blessing."

"Fucker," Dad mumbles. "You had me worried there for a second."

Knowing we have to have this conversation at some point, I say, "Noah and I have been talking. I don't have the patience to work with numbers."

"Do you want to take over from your Uncle Jax?"

I nod. "Do you mind?"

"Not at all." Dad gives me a reassuring smile. "Will Noah then stay on an extra year at Trinity to complete his masters in accounting?"

"Yeah, he's already enrolled."

"Then it's all good."

"Also," I clear my throat, "seeing as I'm graduating, I'll have to look for a place of my own."

"Whaaat?" Dad pretends to be shocked. "You're not coming back home?"

I let out a burst of laughter. "Not a chance."

"Ungrateful little shit," he teases, but then he grows serious again. "Your mom and I will give you and Fallon a house as an engagement present."

"Thanks, Dad." I reach over the space between us and hug him tightly, then I grin. "So, what's our limit?"

Dad begins to laugh. "There's no limit when it comes to my son's first house. Just let me know the price, and I'll transfer the funds to your bank account." Dad thinks for a moment, then he says, "Actually, seeing as you're graduating, I'll transfer an amount that has to last you until your first paycheck."

"If you send me a hundred dollars, I'm telling Mom."

Dad lets out a burst of laughter. "Come on, let's get out of here. I have a date with your mother."

Starting the car, I pull out of the parking area, and I steer us back in the direction of my parents' house.

When I get back to the suite, I go check Fallon's room, but finding it empty, I walk to mine, where I find her curled up on my bed.

I shut the door behind me and lock it before I kick off my shoes. I strip down to my boxers and then crawl onto the bed.

I press a kiss to her healed cheek, and it has her stirring.

"Hey, beautiful," I murmur.

Fallon turns onto her back and stretches out. "Hey, how did it go with your Dad?"

"Good." I push up her shirt and press a kiss to her toned stomach. "We drove around."

"Hmm…" she moans as I push her shirt over her breasts.

"No bra. I like this," I tease before I suck her nipple between my teeth. Pulling back, I take hold of her sweatpants and panties and drag them down her legs. I kiss my way up her body until I reach her shirt and pause to pull it over her head.

When I have Fallon naked, I quickly get rid of my boxers. I part her legs with my lower body, and then I rest my arms on either side of her head. I stare at her beautiful face for a moment before I press my lips to hers, and then I kiss her with all the happiness I feel.

Fallon's arms wrap around me, and her palms brush over my skin until she grabs hold of my ass.

I begin to rub my cock against her clit, and it has Fallon lifting her hips to get closer to me.

I deepen the kiss, my tongue brushing hard strokes against her as I reach down, and positioning myself at her entrance, I push inside with one thrust.

Fallon throws her head back, a gasp rushing over her lips, and then she moans, "God, so good."

My mouth latches onto her throat as I pull out before I drive back into her. Unable to keep the pace slow, my hips speed up, and when Fallon's body begins to tense up beneath mine, I quickly claim her moan with my mouth so the others won't hear us.

I keep thrusting fast and hard, and when I feel Fallon shudder against me, my own orgasm shoots through my body.

We capture each other's moans with a heated kiss, and once our releases fade, I slowly keep pumping into her, not wanting to pull out yet.

Fuck, I wish I could just bury myself permanently inside her. Knowing that's not an option, I reluctantly pull out, and we go clean ourselves up before crawling under the covers. I pull Fallon against me and drop a kiss on her hair as she rests her cheek on my chest.

"Who loves you?" I murmur as I take hold of her hand so I can flatten her palm over my heart.

Fallon lifts her head and rests her chin on my peck. "You."

My eyes lock on hers, and I see my entire world in her golden-brown irises. "Who am I?"

Fallon gives me the most beautiful smile. "Mine."

Yeah, I'm hers, because without her, I'll just cease to exist.

Epilogue

KAO

(Start of summer break)

I check my pocket again to make sure the ring is still there, then glance at the watch on my wrist.

"We're going to be late," Jase yells on my behalf.

Only the guys know I'm proposing to Fallon tonight. They all thought it would be a great surprise for the girls.

"Mila!" Jase yells again.

"What did I do wrong?" Mila shouts back, and a couple of seconds later, she walks into the living room, looking amazing in a royal blue dress Fallon probably forced her to wear.

"Nothing, I'm just calling you," Jase says.

"But you used my name," Mila argues.

"Yeah, that's your name last time I checked," Jase teases her while he wraps his arms around her waist.

"No, you call be Babe. Mila is for when you're upset with me."

I begin to laugh, but it dries up the second my eyes land on Fallon.

"God, woman," I breathe as I drink in the sight of her in a red dress," you're a vision to behold."

"I'll never get tired of you looking at me like that," Fallon teases, and then she holds a necklace out to me. "Help, please."

I take it from her and first brush her hair to the side before I clasp the necklace in place. I press a kiss to her neck, then pull back so I can look at her again.

"Everyone ready?" Jase asks. We all nod. "Good, let's get this show on the road."

Jase and Mila take the lead with Hunter and Jade at the back as we make our way out of the building.

When I open the passenger door to my Aston Martin for Fallon, my eyes drift over her face for any sign that she might be nervous. We've driven together a couple of times, but tonight we're going to The Ranch House, and we're taking the same route the accident happened on.

She gives me a bright smile before she slips into the car.

My gaze scans over the other cars, and I watch as Hana and Noah get into his car.

Then Jase catches my eye, and he gives me a chin lift. "I'll be right in front of you. Don't worry," he assures me.

I turn my head to where Hunter is, and he grins at me. "We've got your back. Let's go."

I climb in behind the wheel, and we first pull on our seat belts. Then I lean over to Fallon, and I press a kiss to her mouth. "You ready?"

"As ready as I'll ever be."

I wait for Jase to pull out of the parking lot before I fall in behind him. Noah and Hunter bring up the rear end of our convoy as we leave the campus grounds.

God, please. Don't let anything go wrong tonight.

Wanting to distract Fallon, I ask, "Have you made a list of houses for us to go view?"

"Yeah, we have two appointments on Sunday."

"Good."

I tighten my grip on the steering wheel, and Fallon must notice because she murmurs, "We're going to be fine."

"Yeah," I whisper as we turn onto the road where the accident happened.

As we near the scene, Jase begins to slow down, and reaching the spot where the truck hit us, he puts on his hazards.

My eyes dart to the rearview mirror, and I notice Noah and Hunter doing the same.

Fallon lets out a shaky breath, and then she covers her mouth as she tries to regain control of her emotions.

"We made it past the accident site," I say.

It finally feels like the past is now behind us and we can one hundred percent focus on our future together.

The minute I stop the car outside the restaurant, Fallon unclasps her seatbelt, and then she darts into my arms.

She holds me tightly, then says, "Thank you for not leaving me." Before I can respond, she presses a kiss to my lips. Pulling back, her eyes shimmer with emotion. "Let's go eat."

When we climb out of the car, Jase lets out a holler. "Let's get this party started."

Walking into the restaurant we reserved just for our group, with the most beautiful woman at my side, there is no doubt in my mind that our love is one of a kind.

FALLON

Trust Kao to reserve the entire restaurant just for us. We all enjoy the fantastic food, and when we're waiting for dessert to come, Kao pushes his chair back and rises to his feet.

When he holds his hand out to me, I ask, "Dance? Now?"

"Come on. Humor me."

I place my hand in his, and we walk to an open space. A familiar song begins to play, and instantly tears push up my throat.

Stand by Me by *John Newman* fills the air, and just like when we danced to it on our first date, I get swept up in Kao's arms.

My eyes never leave Kao's as I listen to the lyrics.

When the song ends, and silence falls around us, a smile tugs at the corner of Kao's mouth. Then he takes a step back, and when he goes down on one knee, pins and needles spread over my entire body as the surprise hits me full force.

"Fallon." I nod like an idiot even though he hasn't even asked me anything yet, and it makes his smile grow. Then Kao pulls a ring out of his breast pocket, and holding it to me, he says, "Facing a day without your beauty in it will be worse than being blind." Tears well in my eyes, and I struggle to keep them back so I can see his face. "Facing a

347

day without hearing your voice will be worse than being deaf. Facing a day without you will be my end because my heart only beats for you. Will you marry me?"

When I nod, Kao climbs to his feet. His eyes lock on mine. "To answer your question, yes, I will still love you when you're old and wrinkly."

A sob flutters over my lips, and throwing my arms around his neck, I bury my face against him. "You remember?"

"Sorry, it took me so long to answer you."

I shake my head, and pulling back, I fan my face with my hand. "Now, let me see the ring."

Everyone starts to laugh.

Kao slips a princess cut diamond onto my finger, and the rock gleams in the electric light above us.

"Now you're finally mine," Kao murmurs.

Shaking my head, I smile up at him. "I've always been yours."

The End.

Want to read where it all started?

Go 1 Click HEARTLESS.

And when you're done with the Enemies To Lovers Series,

follow it up with Trinity Academy.

All the sale links are listed in the back matter of the book.

The Heirs

Reading order of future releases:

Coldhearted Heir
Novel #1
Hunter Chargill (*Mason and Kingsley's son*)
&
Jade Daniels (*Rhett & Evie's daughter*)

Arrogant Heir
Novel #2
Jase Reyes – (*Julian & Jamie's son*)
&
Mila West – (*Logan & Mia's Daughter*)

Defiant Heir
Novel #3
Kao Reed (*Marcus and Willow's son*)
&
Fallon Reyes (*Falcon & Layla's daughter*)

Loyal Heir
Novel #4
Forest Reyes (*Falcon & Layla's son*)
&
Aria Chargill (*Mason & Kingsley's daughter*)

Callous Heir
Novel #5
Noah West (*Jaxson & Leigh's son*)
&
Carla Reyes (*Julian & Jamie's daughter*)

<u>Sinful Heir</u>
Novel #6
Tristan Hayes (*Carter & Della's son*)
&
Hana Cutler (*Lake & Lee's daughter*)

<u>Tempted Heir</u>
Novel #7
Christopher Hayes (*Carter & Della's son*)
&
Dash West (*Jaxson & Leigh's daughter*)

<u>Forbidden Heir</u>
Novel #8
Ryker West (*Logan & Mia's son*)
&
Danny Hayes (*Carter & Della's daughter*)

Stand Alone High School Romance

Black Mountain Academy Series

<u>Not My Hero</u>
Colton Lawson
(Brady from Coldhearted Heir's Brother.)
&
Brie Weinstock
(daughter of Serena from Trinity Academy)

Trinity Academy

FALCON
Novel #1
Falcon Reyes & Layla Shepard

MASON
Novel #2
Mason Chargill & Kingsley Hunt

LAKE
Novel #3
Lake Cutler & Lee-ann Park

JULIAN
Novel #4
A Stand Alone Novel
Julian Reyes (*Falcon's Brother*)
&
Jamie Truman (*Della's Sister – Heartless, TETLS*)

THE EPILOGUE
A Trinity Academy Novella

Enemies To Lovers

Heartless
Novel #1
Carter Hayes & Della Truman

Reckless
Novel #2
Logan West & Mia Daniels

Careless
Novel #3
Jaxson West & Leigh Baxter

Ruthless
Novel #4
Marcus Reed & Willow Brooks

Shameless
Novel #5
Rhett Daniels & Evie Cole

False Perceptions
Novel #6
A Stand Alone Novel
Hayden Cole *(Evie's Dad)*

Connect with me

Newsletter

FaceBook

Amazon

GoodReads

BookBub

Instagram

Twitter

Website

About the author

Michelle Heard is a Wall Street Journal, and USA Today Bestselling Author who loves creating stories her readers can get lost in. She resides in South Africa with her son where she's always planning her next book to write, and trip to take.

Want to be up to date with what's happening in Michelle's world? Sign up to receive the latest news on her alpha hero releases → <u>NEWSLETTER</u>

If you enjoyed this book or any book, please consider leaving a review. It's appreciated by authors.

Acknowledgments

Kao's story would not have been possible without my amazing reader, *Donita Burgess*. Girl, your strength left me speechless and inspired. Thank you for all your advice and guidance throughout the book.

To my alpha and beta readers, Sherrie, Sheena, Allyson. Kelly, Elaine, Sarah, and Leeann – Thank you for being the godparents of my paper-baby.

My street team – you're the best!!! Thank you so much for promoting my books.

Candi Kane PR - Thank you for being patient with me and my bad habit of missing deadlines. (I'm working on fixing that bad habit wink-wink)

Sybil – Thank you for giving my paper-babies the perfect look.

To my readers, thank you for loving these characters as much as I do.

A special thank you to every blogger and reader who took the time to take part in the cover reveal and release day.

Love ya all tons ;)

Made in United States
Troutdale, OR
11/18/2024

24991747R00199